CW01090849

THE TUDOR SISTERS

THE TUDOR SISTERS

Aileen Armitage

This title first published in Great Britain 2005 by
SEVERN HOUSE PUBLISHERS LTD of
9–15 High Street, Sutton, Surrey SM1 1DF.
Originally published in 1974 in Great Britain under
the title *Court Cadenza* and pseudonym *Aileen Quigley*.
This title first published in the USA 2005 by
SEVERN HOUSE PUBLISHERS INC of
595 Madison Avenue, New York, N.Y. 10022.

British Library Cataloguing in Publication Data

Armitage, Aileen
    The Tudor sisters
    1.   Boleyn, Mary, 1508-1543 - Fiction
    2.   Anne Boleyn, Queen, consort of Henry VIII,
         King of England, 1507-1536 - Fiction
    3.   Henry, VIII, King of England, 1491-1547 -
         Relations with women - Fiction
    4.   Sisters - England - History - 16th century - Fiction
    5.   Great Britain - Henry VIII, 1509-1547 - Fiction
    6.   Historical fiction
    I.   Title
    823.9'14 [F]

    ISBN 0-7278-6250-2

Printed and bound in Great Britain by
MPG Books Ltd., Bodmin, Cornwall.

For Evelyn Armitage,
my mother

CHAPTER ONE

AUBADE

THERE was no doubt of it, Mother was dying. Mary Boleyn, with all the solemn gravity of her twelve years, hunched thin arms round bony knees as she sat alone in a secluded corner of the castle gardens and reflected miserably that despite all the adults' silence on the subject, her beautiful mother was obviously on the brink of death, and nothing Mary could say or do would save her.

It was nothing they had said, neither the servants nor her normally ebullient father Thomas, nor even the usually loquacious governess Simonette, but rather the hushed, respectful manner in which they all went about their business, tiptoeing about the castle with fingers laid to lips. Not, Mary knew, to avoid disturbing the new babe her mother had recently borne with such pain, for the little mite had not survived more than a few hours; but from the constant, agitated visits of the physician and the mutterings and shaking of heads Mary guessed that the delicate Elizabeth Howard lay in the grip of childbed fever, from which few ever recovered.

She leaned her forehead against her knees, feeling the late summer sun lapping against the nape of her neck where it filtered through the latticework of apple trees. It was so bitterly unfair that the sun should shine so benevolently, wrapping the vast gardens in its warmth and promise of life, while up there in the castle her mother lay pale and fighting for breath to cling to her short life.

All summer long there had been joy and expectancy in the air as Mary and her older brother George and young

Anne had revelled in the prospect of a new baby brother. Never once had it occurred to their young optimistic minds that aught untoward could happen, either to the babe or to their mother, and of all three children Mary had anticipated the coming of the child most eagerly.

'It will be a boy, I feel it,' Anne had pronounced solemnly, sitting boyishly in the low branches of an apple tree while George teased her, tickling her nose with a plume of grass.

'How can you be so sure, little sister?' he had asked, pausing in his game to eye her questioningly.

'I just know, as I always know these things,' Anne replied gravely, her dark eyes sober and far away, and George had nodded understandingly. Neither he nor Mary believed the village children, who were convinced Anne was a witch-child and shied nervously at her coming, but there was undoubtedly something strange about her worldly wisdom, child of ten though she was. It was almost as though the fairies had sprinkled her with magic dust, the way she could see through people and put her finger uncannily accurately on their true feelings, and even sometimes to foresee events. Mary, convinced of a little brother's arrival, had waited impatiently for the child who was to be her soul-mate as George was Anne's.

Not that Mary was jealous — Heaven forbid! But just sometimes it was a little lonely and envy-provoking to watch George's head and Anne's bent close in private colloquy, not deliberately shutting her out but simply so absorbed in each other as to be unaware of her existence. Despite the difference in their ages — George now fourteen and on the verge of manhood, and Anne still a child — they seemed magnetically drawn to each other, confiding their hopes and troubles in each other as they never did in Mary.

So the new babe was to make up for it, to be Mary's own close friend, a being to cherish and watch over. She would encourage his first tentative steps and laughingly reassure him when he stumbled. Naturally he would turn to her to entrust her with his childish confidences, and soon they would have the intimacy between them that bound George and Anne invisibly, yet undeniably close.

But now the yearned for brother was not to be. And as if Fate did not consider the blow cruel enough, her mother was to be wrenched from her too. Mary brushed away the tears hovering on her lashes; it was selfish to feel sad on her own account, desolate though she would feel. Anne and George too would be bereft and anguished, and poor Father! He was proud indeed of his beautiful, coveted wife and of her high breeding, so much better-born than himself. He, too, would be lost without the lovely Lady Elizabeth.

A sob rose unbidden in Mary's throat. Oh Mother! How can I ever hope to replace you? Much as I shall try to comfort Father and guide Anne as you would have done, who is to help succour me?

Soft voices murmuring caused Mary to raise her head and gaze across the sunlit lawns through a misted veil of tears. George, his head bent to listen attentively, walked hand in hand with Anne towards the herb garden on the way back to the castle. Mary drew back into the shade of the tree, unwilling to be caught thus weeping, and hoping the green of her gown merging into the undergrowth would conceal her from view.

They disappeared from sight, deep still in conversation. The sun's heat lessened on Mary's bowed shoulders and the shadows of the castle lengthened across the lawns, casting a purple mantle over the rich green. Pollen-sated bees droned homeward and butterflies clustering over the lilac bushes dwindled and fled. Mary gazed about her at the profuse beauty of the gardens, at the blossoms spilling over from the stone urns on the terraces, their deep-hued petals crimson in the evening light, and was unfathomably saddened. Soon they would be calling her to break the sad news, unaware that grief had already pierced her young heart and engulfed her in terrible, vulnerable isolation.

'Mary, Mary!'

She did not lift her head from her knees though she heard Anne's clear young voice well enough. Soon George's gruffer call was added to the childish treble, but still Mary did not move. The voices faded, and Mary sat on under the tree, lost in misery, until evening's chill breezes made her shiver. She rose slowly and stretched her stiff limbs to ease the discomfort, but nothing could ease the ache in her heart.

Mademoiselle Simonette, the governess, glowered at Mary for her belated arrival at supper, and waved her thin hands expressively in disapproval. Mary ignored the reproof and instead searched the governess's angry dark eyes for news.

'My lady mother, Simonette? How is she?'

The governess's mouth snapped shut. Her gaze shot quickly to where her other two charges sat already at table, and she frowned. Anne looked up.

Mary saw the embarrassment in the Frenchwoman's eyes as the child's dark, innocent gaze questioned hers. Simonette looked away sharply; then she caught sight of George, leaning on his elbows and was swift to grasp the means of escape.

'Master George! Your elbows! Do you hope to be accepted at the Court of His Majesty with the manners of a ploughboy! And you, mistress Anne, slouching like a milkmaid! Sit up now, back straight as I taught you! You too may go to join your father at Court one day, and your manners must be as impeccable as the Queen's if you hope to do so. Come, sit down by me, Mary.'

White-faced, Mary sat but could not eat. Mademoiselle's refusal to reply had answered her question more eloquently than words. A ball of hard, cold ice in her stomach made her feel sickened and faint.

'Come now, Mary, you must eat,' Simonette protested, drawing forward a bowl of dessert. 'See here, the cook has prepared your favourite, roast quinces covered in thick cream. How lucky you are! No doubt she thinks it is your birthday, to spoil you so!'

But despite well-meant persuasion and banter, Mary could not eat. Anne and George, in happy ignorance, raised their eyebrows and ate with gusto.

Far into the night Mary lay awake and listened to Anne's regular breathing as she slept, her thin little body curled trustingly against Mary's in their big feather bed. Anne had not seen Simonette's finger laid warningly to her pursed lips as she and Mary bade their governess good-night, but Mary had understood the unspoken advice and during the girls' drowsy bedtime talk she had made no mention to her younger sister of her fears. Not even when Anne, her little face seriously suddenly, had broken off the chatter to gasp, 'Oh Mary! We did not say good-night to Father! I haven't seen him all day and I forgot he was at home, so often he is away in London!'

'Never mind,' Mary reassured her. 'He has been with Mother, entertaining her while she lies abed. He would not thank us to disturb him.

Reassured, Anne had talked dreamily of this and that till sleep overcame her. And now, in the warm stillness of the night, Mary lay feeling miserably alone. Alone in the secret knowledge of her mother's dying, and desperately alone at the prospect of losing her. Mother, so warm and vibrant and full of life and love, would soon be snapped off, swiftly and irrevocably, like a winter icicle on the eaves, brittle and irreplaceable. And there would be no one to make up for her warmth; not Anne nor George, so all-in-all to each other, and certainly not Father, distant and brusque and forever absorbed in his important business on the King, his master's behalf. So earnestly involved he was in these great matters that he spent far more time in London, with King Harry at Greenwich or Westminster, than ever he did here in Hever or in their other home Blickling Hall in Norfolk. Father was a shadowy figure with an air of absorption and the continual lines of preoccupation on his bearded face, far removed from the loving, open-armed creature that Mother was. And Simonette, with her precise Gallic insistence on trivial detail, had not a jot of maternal feeling in her desiccated body. Warm tears flowed as Mary mourned.

Suddenly Anne's thin frame shuddered and she sat upright, staring wide-eyed into the gloom about the bed. Mary put a protective arm about her shivering body.

'What is it, Anne? Surely you are not cold on such a warm night?'

'I am frightened, Mall.' Anne's voice was timid and her little pointed face glowing white in the grey-violet light of dawn.

'A nightmare, sweetheart?'

'I know not. Only that I am frightened, and oh! so cold, Mall! Cuddle me, I am so afraid!!

Anne continued to moan softly as Mary's arms enfolded her and her soft voice murmured soothing words of comfort. But the far-away gaze in Anne's eyes as she had started awake agitated Mary. Anne, with her strange powers of prevision, had sensed death in the air, Mary felt certain, just as she herself did. No sooner had her young sister's troubled eyes at last closed again in sleep than a swish of skirts and the closing of the chamber door disturbed once again the stillness of the dawn.

Simonette's thin, angular body bent over the bed. 'Mary, are you awake? Come swiftly, child, for your lady mother would see you. Do not waken Anne.'

Mary withdrew her arms carefully from about her sister's sleeping body, rose and put on her bedgown. Simonette waited impatiently outside the door to lead the way through the dark corridors of the castle to Lady

Elizabeth's bed-chamber.

Sir Thomas, still dressed and standing grey-faced within the circle of candlelight that illuminated the canopied bed, nodded curtly to his daughter and left the chamber abruptly with Simonette. Mary approached the bed apprehensively, drawing back the hangings to see her mother more clearly. Lady Elizabeth lay, spectre-pale and motionless, only the once-lustrous eyes moving restlessly in her ashen face. She lifted a limp hand to take hold of Mary's fingers and draw her closer. Mary gazed in horror at the gaunt face, its beauty fled and the limp fair curls clinging damply to the sweat-soaked brow, and shuddered at the coldness of her mother's touch, the chill of death already in her fingertips.

'Come closer, child.' The words, whispered with effort, hovered tenuously on the dawn air like fleeting will-o'-the-wisps. Mary bent low, her unbound hair falling over the dying woman's breast. Lady Elizabeth entwined her fingers in its silky mesh.

'Beloved Mary, I am so afraid for you when I am gone.'

Her daughter fought back the lump that rose in her throat, and forbade the tears to fall.

'Fear not for me, Mother. Nor for Anne, for I shall care for her.'

A faint smile flickered on the sheet-white face. 'It is not for Anne I fret, my child, for she is old beyond her years and worldly-wise. Morever she has George to protect her, but you, with your vulnerable heart, little one, you have no one.'

She laid a cold finger on Mary's lips to stay the protesting words. 'I know you are older than she, and more able in the house, but you have not your sister's single-mindedness and ambition. For all she is so young, it is already clear that Anne knows her own mind. She is clever and quick, and will turn all things to her purpose. But you, my sweet, you are prettier than she yet you will find life harder, for you are so unsubtle, so pliable and anxious to please. I fear for you, my precious, for you will be an easy prey to others' ambition.'

Pausing, she took several shallow breaths before continuing. 'Anne and George will carve their own destinies, Mary, to whatever end it may lead. But you, with your warmth and love for your fellow men, you will be as clay in others' hands if you do not take a care. You need guidance, and since I shall not be here to help you . . . '

Her voice faded away into the lightening gloom, and Mary felt the cold fingers tighten on her hand. 'Marry soon, my child,' the faint voice added in a whisper. 'Choose wisely and marry young. You have need of a strong arm to guide you.'

Lady Elizabeth's head rolled to one side and her eyes closed. Mary's eyes misted with tears as her father and Simonette hastened into the chamber.

'She is wearied from talking and must sleep,' Sir Thomas pronounced gruffly. 'Return to your room, Mary, but have a care not to disturb Anne.'

As Simonette led her from the stillness of the chamber, Mary knew her Mother's sleep would be the eternal slumber of death and in the darkness of the corridor she sobbed unrestrainedly into Simonette's unyielding shoulder.

'Come now, mistress Mary, pull yourself together,' Simonette exhorted in her crispest tones. 'Dry your tears and return to bed for a time.'

But as Mary clambered cautiously into the great bed, carefully avoiding Anne's sleeping figure, the tears fell fast. By the time she arose again, Lady Elizabeth would be no more than a cherished memory.

CHAPTER TWO

PASTORALE

THE pain and anguish of Lady Elizabeth's untimely death gradually receded from the Boleyn household, leaving the castle a little greyer for the loss of her vivacious beauty. In time the wound healed for little Anne and even for Mary, though she still felt a twist of nostalgic pain from time to time.

After the funeral obsequies when Lady Elizabeth's body had been laid to rest in the Howard mausoleum at Lambeth, Father returned at once to his duties at Court and before long he sent for George to join him in London on train as a page. Secretly Mary found joy in her brother's departure, much as she loved him, for now the greatest barrier between herself and Anne was removed. Now, perhaps, in their solitude they would draw closer together and draw comfort from each other.

But she had not bargained for Aunt Wyatt's determination to replace their lost mother. Hardly a day passed but Aunt Wyatt came over to Hever from nearby Allington ton Castle, bringing with her cousin Tom and cousin Meg to keep the Boleyn children company.

'There now, you and Tom are much of an age, and so are Anne and Meg.' Aunt Wyatt said cheerfully to Mary, convinced that all would work out well. but, contrary to her expectation, it was towards Anne that Tom gravitated, his smiling gaze lighting on Mary only briefly before darting past her to her sloe-eyed serious sister. Within minutes he would sweep Anne away into some private game, leaving Mary to occupy little Meg as best she could. Nevertheless,

Mary welcomed her cousins' company, for their laughter and bright chatter helped to dispel the last traces of gloom from Hever Castle.

Father came home briefly during the twelve days of Christmas, to bring them all gifts and news from Court, but his heavy manner and tart demands from Simonette as to their progress in the schoolroom filled Mary with dismay.

'Mistress Anne progresses well, my lord,' Simonette replied with a nod of approval to her favourite charge, 'but Mistress Mary . . .' She paused and spread her bony hands in an expressive gesture, her thin shoulders raised in a disowning shrug.

'Mary makes little headway?' Sir Thomas's grave and furrowed brow caused Mary to tremble. She could not help it if her wits were slower to comprehend those tortuous French verbs than Anne's quicksilver mind, but she hated to disappoint her father.

'She tries, my lord,' Simonette assured him, 'but if the ability is not there . . .'

'She must try harder,' Sir Thomas retorted, and turned away. Mary regarded his averted back sadly. So it had ever been, the smile for Anne and the reprimand for herself. It was of no avail that she could sew a finer seam than Anne, or practised hours longer than her impatient sister on the harpsichord. For her demanding father only the aptitudes of the brain were to be applauded, and there her mercurial sister had the advantage of her.

But soon, with a flurry of final orders and a clatter of hooves on the courtyard, Sir Thomas was gone again about his courtly business and Hever reverted to its earlier quietness. Between Aunt Wyatt's visits and the hectic games of *cache-cache* in the gloom of wainscoted, panelled corridors and high in the long gallery, Simonette gathered up her charges and bore them away to drill them mercilessly in the intricacies of French syntax and the skills of deportment. Nor must their practice at the harpsichord or the embroidery sampler be allowed to be curtailed by so much as a minute, simply because the master was from home; rather must Simonette labour the harder with her pupils so that Sir Thomas should be well aware of their progress on his return.

'Come now Anne, smaller steps if you please, and a straight back as you make your reverence,' Simonette would exhort as the two maidens practised the courtly walk and curtsey that was expected of them. And in the schoolroom Mary drew the benefit of Simonette's sharp tongue.

'Why do you not listen, mademoiselle, as your sister does? I have no need to repeat my words for Mistress Anne. Now, *parlons en français un peu* . . .'

But Mary's mind could not focus on Mademoiselle's words. It was so hard to concentrate on complex matters of the mind when the eye was distracted by more interesting, worldly things, the bumble bee hovering threateningly above Simonette's well-coiffed head, the lustre of smooth black hair on the nape of Anne's bent head and the chatter of blackbirds on the sunlit lawns outside. It was no use, The world of the senses held far more appeal for her than that of the mind.

Thus it was with an immense feeling of relief that she left the schoolroom at last, flinging her books aside to hasten to see if cousin Tom had arrived. But always his gaze sought out Anne, her eyes still misty in thought from Simonette's teaching.

'Come, little Anne, I have a paper to show you,' he would say, drawing Anne aside to the privacy of an arbour or the shade of a spreading oak, while Mary, forlorn yet resigned, would be left to show little Meg the delights of the cool, flagged dairy or the secrets of the stillroom.

There was sensuous gratification even in this, Mary reflected philosophically, for she delighted in the delicious scent of fresh milk and the luxurious texture of the thick cream tumbling in the butter churner, and the stillroom yielded yet more pleasure. One could open jars of herbs to sniff, or precious bottles of rose and lavender water and feel Meg's chubby hand in hers stiffen as she squealed with disgust at the smell of fermenting wine. The little maid's company afforded Mary a soothing sense of calm and warmth, and she daydreamed of the life she herself would probably lead one day as the mistress of just such a household, the wife of some country knight perhaps, with laughing, affectionate children like Meg. She had so much love inside her, burning to be lavished, and yet no one on whom to lavish it — yet.

Strangely enough it was Anne, old beyond her tender years, who first broached the subject of love and marriage one evening after the tiring-maid had turned back the bedcovers and bade them good-night. In the twilight dimness of their chamber Anne peered hard at her reflection in her silver hand-mirror, twisting her head this way and that to inspect her profile, then clicked her tongue impatiently and laid the mirror aside.

'In truth, Mary, I wonder sometimes why you should be so fair and wholesome and I so dark and ill-favoured. Who would credit we were born of the same mother? Think you a handsome man would ever wish to wed such an unfortunately-endowed creature as I? Shall I be a lonely old maid when you are wed and surrounded by babes?'

Mary laughed good-naturedly. 'Not you, Nan. Your wit and lively nature more than compensate for any misfortunes you imagine, and imagination is surely your undoing for you are indeed comely.'

'I am dark-skinned, Mall, sallow as curdled milk.'

'Your skin is creamy, sweetheart, and that blends well with your black hair, straight and smooth as a yard of pumpwater. See how mine curls defiantly, however hard I brush it. I shall never be in fashion.'

'But you are so pretty, Mall!'

'As are you, my sweeting. See, in the mirror. See how alike in feature we are? The same shape of nose and mouth? The same line of chin and jaw? The difference lies only in our colouring, Nan, your dark eyes and my blue, and in our hair.'

'You are beautiful, Mall, just like Mother was. A picture of roseland gilt whom men will worship and yearn to possess. I am thin and dark. There is no wonder the village children call me a witch-child.' Flinging herself on the bed Anne sank her pointed chin dispiritedly into her cupped hands, her slanted dark eyes growing misty. Mary sought for words of reassurance.

'Because of your bewitching ways, sweetheart, the way you attract people on account of your cleverness and wit. Why, Tom Wyatt cannot bear to be parted from you. He has no time for a dull creature alike me, however pretty!'

A prick of envy lay behind Mary's words, but at the moment comfort for Anne was her prime concern. Not so very long ago she could remember being thin and angular herself and wishing for the day she would become rounded and blossom as a woman. Nature was now remedying the defect, as in time it would for Anne.

At the mention of Tom Wyatt's name Anne had rolled over on to her back, and lay now gazing at the bed-canopy above her. A smile curved her lips.

'Cousin Tom wrote a poem today.'

'Another?' queried Mary. 'I vow he is becoming a regular poet, so much he versifies these days.'

'But this was for me, Mall, specially for me.' Anne's voice was low and vibrant with contentment now, all trace gone of the anguish of a minute earlier. Mary was quick to turn the information to Anne's benefit.

'There now, Nan, a tribute from a young man, to a maid who considers herself plain. How can you say you are not beautiful?'

Anne swung her long thin legs over the side of the high

bed and squealed pleasurably. 'Cousin Tom is but a youth, Mall, not a man yet. But it *is* flattering to have a poem written to one. He bade me keep it a secret, but I shall let you read it.'

She clambered down and crossed to the chest to fetch a sheet of paper from a drawer. She looked oddly frail and vulnerable in her nightshift, thought Mary pensively and could not resist a surge of protective love as her younger sister stood before her, toes curling into the depths of a skin rug, as she offered her sister the paper.

'It is a sonnet,' she said shyly, 'yet unpolished, but I think it has merit. Tom has such a clever way of using words, like a painter building up a picture. Read it and tell me what you think.'

She hung anxiously, finger in mouth, as Mary took it, watching her sister's face to gauge her reaction. Mary read the first few lines in silence, trying to hide the embarrassment that flooded her for the poem was undoubtedly of love, and no innocent love at that.

'Where have you got to? Read it aloud to me,' Anne interrupted at last. Mary murmured the last few lines of the sonnet aloud, while Anne stood with hands clasped, smiling.

> 'Throw wide thy casement, lift thy face
> And let sweet lovelight, like the blessed rain,
> Enswathe thee in suffusing grace
> Ere autumn comes, drawing chill winter in its train.
> For man must pluck the blossoms, it to save,
> Else Death the eternal Bridegroom i' the grave.'

'There!' Anne breathed ecstatically. 'Is that not beautiful, Mall?'

Mary lifted a troubled face. 'It is not, I think, a fitting poem for a maid to receive, Nan,' she said hesitantly, biting her lip and wondering how best to explain to her sister.

Anne snatched the paper from her hand.

'You do not appreciate it! I told you it was yet unfinished, yet you would criticise rhyme and scan without regard for poor Tom's effort!' Anne's face crumpled in misery, near to tears, and she flung herself angrily into bed, the paper crumpling under her vexed hand. Mary pinched out the candle and crawled in beside her.

'I am sorry, Nan, I did not mean to sound unkind, for in truth you were right to say Tom is clever with words. I have no doubt he will be a fine poet one day, one England will remember with pride.'

Anne's stiff back relaxed.

'And I am happy he dedicates his verse to you, sweetheart. You must be very proud and happy.'

Mary could feel Anne's head nodding agreement, then her small voice came out of the darkness. 'But I do not think I shall marry him, Mall.'

'Marry him? Mary could not attempt to conceal her surprise.

'Yes. He says he wants to marry me.'

'But — but you are not yet twelve years old, Nan!'

'Nevertheless he is certain. I am not so sure.'

Mary was too aghast to reply. For some moments she turned the thought over in her mind, and it was Anne who spoke first.

'I told Tom he must not be so determined, for I am certain Father has other plans for us. No doubt he has already determined our husbands for us. Not that I shall marry where Father decrees unless it is to my own liking.'

Mary was dumbfounded. Anne's voice held such determination for one so young, but what amazed her yet more was that her young sister was already so aware of their father's nature. His possible choice of husbands for them had never seriously crossed Mary's serene mind. She leaned over and regarded Anne's dim, recumbent figure anxiously.

'Think you Father will — choose husbands for us?'

Anne snorted. 'He will. Simonette says it is usual for

one in his station, since Father is a knight now, and since he has daughters born with noble blood from our mother's family, it is certain he will barter well for us.'

Mary cogitated over her words. 'Father loves us, Nan; he will do what is best for us,' she said uncertainly. Anne sat upright, her dark eyes hollow and luminous in the eerie paleness of her face.

'No doubt what is best for him,' she said in low, emphatic tones. 'But with the breeding that is our inheritance from the one side of our family, allied with the shrewd wit of the merchant side, I am certain we can go far by ourselves. My choice of a husband will be mine alone, Mall, of that I can assure you.'

Then, with the untroubled innocence of a child Anne turned over and settled herself to sleep, leaving Mary to wonder at and admire the forcefulness of her words. Within minutes Anne was deeply asleep, but Mary had much to occupy her mind, her thoughts racing over the new matters to which Anne had unwittingly given rise.

Firstly, there was the matter of Father's plans for them and how he might venture to secure his own advance through politic marriages. It was a business he knew well, for had he not bettered his own merchant stature by taking to wife the niece of the Duke of Norfolk? He would do no less for the children of whom he was so proud and on whom he had lavished such splendid education, for his business acumen had taught him how to invest his money wisely. Anne's surmising was no doubt correct, but since Mary just could not envisage how this might be achieved she soon abandoned the thought to take up instead one that was closer to her heart: Tom Wyatt's sonnet to Anne. She had always known Tom admired Anne and sought her individed attention, but an open declaration of love and the intention to marry . . . Yet no man sought the favour of the older and allegedly more beautiful sister. Again Mary felt the pangs of frustration. So much love clamoured within her breast, mixed with a yearning to be cradled and cosseted in the warmth of another's arms, yet it was Anne, a mere child, whom another sought.

A silent tear fell soundlessly to the pillow. Anne slept on unheeding.

It was a still, sultry afternoon when Simonette, fluttering her fingertips to her forehead and complaining of a ghastly headache on account of the heat, dismissed the girls from the schoolroom bidding them go rest, and read a while before supper. Anne took a sheaf of Tom's papers to read in privacy in the arbour beyond the lawns, and Mary, donning a little linen cap to protect her head from the sun's heat and an ancient, faded gown, set off to saunter through the orchards and away into the meadows beyond. The stream, rippling haphazardly over the stones, made a trilling, cooling sound and Mary wandered on along the bank, downstream towards the village. It was a day of perfect beauty and stillness, butterflies hovering almost motionless over the wild flowers as though too drowsy to move, and the air breathed calm and contentment. But Mary could find no contentment. Her heart ached to share the bliss of such perfection, to find a soul-mate with whom to savour the day's luxuriance, for while her senses responded to its brilliance, she knew it was all too transient.

With a sigh she seated herself on the stream's grassy bank and, pulling off her mules, she dipped her toes into the cool comfort of its waters. A swishing sound behind her made her turn her head, but there was naught to be seen save a tall hedgerow. Presently, through a gap in the hedge a fair, tousled head appeared, and a village lad of some seventeen summers stood akimbo before her, a short-handled scythe in his fist. Mary flushed, aware of her hot. dishevelled appearance and her unladylike attitude. The youth tossed the scythe aside and sprawled beside her, thrusting his filthy bare feet into the stream.

'Lord, but it's hot,' he commented with a contented

sigh. Mary noted the warmth and humour in his voice, and the quizzical, interested gaze in his keen blue eyes. 'New about here, ain't you?' he queried, cocking his head to one side.

Mary hesitated. If he were a boy from the village he obviously did not recognise her and would be humiliated to know he had addressed a lady from the castle in such a familiar manner. Not wanting to lose a God-given companion so hastily she decided to speak only half the truth.

'My home is in Norfolk,' she confided softly. Well, it was partly true; the family *did* spend part of the year at Blickling Hall.

'Ah, that accounts for why you talk different,' the youth replied, satisfied. He scooped up a cupped handful of stream water and sucked it noisily; Mary regarded his brawny brown arms and broad shoulders with interest. His hair curled crisply about his brow, beaded with sweat and she watched his movements as he dashed more water against his face and then mopped it with his forearm. Then he lay on his hip and curled comfortably beside her. his eyes again intent on her face.

'You don't live in the village,' he commented laconically. 'What are you doing here?'

'I'm — I'm gathering herbs, to take up to the castle.'

'Ah, you're a kitchen wench there, eh?'

Mary nodded. After all, she didn't actually *say* she was, so it wasn't really telling lies.

CHAPTER THREE

TREMOLO

MARY pulled off her linen cap, letting her hair tumble in a golden cloud about her shoulders, revelling in the glorious, abandoned sense of freedom, and turned up her face to the sun's warmth. Her companion was eyeing her thoughtfully.

'You're a comely wench,' he observed at length. 'Much prettier than the other girls in the village.'

'Thank you.' Mary, unaccustomed to male compliments, blushed with pleasure and looked downwards shyly. He sat regarding her downcast lashes with interest.

'What's your name?'

'Mall. And yours?'

'Rafe.' His fingers stole silently across the grass to touch hers, outstretched beside her. Mary trembled involuntarily. The touch of his calloused, work-roughened fingertips on hers sent shudders quivering through her frame. He glanced up at her face with a puzzled look. 'Your hands are soft, Mall, like a lady's'

Mary bit her lip in perplexity, wondering how best to explain away the absence of toil-marks. Oh, that she had Anne's quick brain! A sudden idea occurred. 'I have unguents, given me by my mistress. They are a marvellous remedy for roughened hands.'

Rafe nodded, satisfied. He rolled over on to his back, one hand behind his head and the other extended to reach for a stray curl of Mary's hair that danced in the breeze.

'Beautiful hair,' he murmured appraisingly. 'like the princesses in the fairy tales my mother used to tell me.

Just like a princess you are, Mall, with your hair the colour of ripe corn, and your soft hands and sweet voice.'

His voice, low and vibrant, sent shudders through her, a glow of pure pleasure that he found delight in the sight of her, and her responsive nature was quick to warm and to react to his praise.

'You too have a gentle face, full of humour and compassion,' she said shyly, and saw his eyes widen in surprise. Belatedly she realised her mistake; no village wench would speak so. She hung her head in embarrassment.

Rafe lay silent, his hand still entwined in her long hair. In the quiet of the late afternoon Mary could hear the homeward humming of the bees and the quick splash of a kingfisher in the stream. Then slowly, firmly, Rafe's hold on her tightened and he drew her resolutely down towards him. She relaxed and lay back in the warm grass, watching his other hand steal out from under his head and encircle her waist, his fair head bending over hers. Mary closed her eyes.

His lips were urgent and searching on hers and a boundless joy surged through her. Warmth and responsiveness from a fellow human being; this was what she had sought for so long and been denied. She answered his kisses eagerly, and felt his young body harden against hers with the suppressed tension of an animal sensing its freedom. He disentangled his fingers from her hair and searched instead for her bodice-laces, fumbling with them till they loosened, then probing eagerly inside. Mary felt her flesh leap to meet the strong fingertips, and the mourning and desolation of the past twelve months began to melt away in the ardent warmth of emotion. For Rafe, who showed his feelings for her so demonstrably, she felt a stirring of ardour and affection she had never felt before. Her arms encircling his broad young back, she savoured the rough, sensuous feel of his coarse smock and the tensed muscles beneath.

Suddenly Rafe jerked away and stiffened as he listened intently. Cowbells were tinkling faintly in the distance,

and he groaned. Cursing under his breath and rising an-
steadily to his feet he brushed himself free of the fronds
of grass and fern clinging to his smock and mumbled apologetically. 'Milking time again, Mall. I must go before the
master starts asking questions. Can you meet me tonight,
by the old oak at the crossroads?'

'I — I don't know. I shall try.' Mary's answer was stumbling and irresolute, disappointment mingling with uncertainty. The closeness, the intimate warmth and communion
that had existed between them a moment ago was shattered,
and the delicious sensation of being cared for and admired
was gone. It was cruel to be robbed of such ecstasy so
swiftly. Before Mary could summon the wits to debate how
she could possibly escape Simonette's hawk-like super-
vision to meet him, he was scrambling through the gap
again, and with a swift wave and a smile he was gone.

The sun was dipping low behind the old oak trees surrounding the castle, throwing long shadows across the velvet
lawn as Mary re-traced her steps. Despite the sudden, disappointing wrench from her admirer's arms, Mary's naturally sunny disposition quickly reasserted itself. For the first
time in her young life she had met uninhibited affection
and enjoyed an embrace as warmly given as her own, and
she revelled in the sense of freedom and passion. This
was how she was meant to love, loving and giving, express
ing friendship tangibly and visibly, natural as her God-
given feelings intended her to be, she felt certain. She
could not resist humming excitedly as she mounted the
stone steps. If not tonight, then tomorrow or some other
day she and Rafe would enjoy that closeness again. Mary
hugged the secret prospect joyfully to her bosom.

Lightheartedly tripping up the castle steps Mary almost
collided with the silent dark figure of Simonette, standing
gaunt and stark as a gargoyle at the top. Thin fingers darted out to grasp Mary's shoulder reprovingly.

'*Tiens, mademoiselle,* this is no way to conduct yourself,

hurling yourself upstairs like some village hoyden! Grace and dignity at all times, as I have repeatedly told you.'

Her sharp, high voice was accompanied by a critical gaze, Simonette's keen dark eyes traversing Mary's figure from the gilt tendrils escaping from her cap, down the dusty, crumpled gown, to the muddied mules on her feet. Her white brow furrowed in dismayed concern.

'*Bon Dieu, Marie, qu'est-ce que vous est arrivé, mon enfant?* Where have you been all afternoon?' Her eyes narrowed to gleaming slits. Mary fidgeted uncomfortably. Lying and deceit had no part in her nature, but to admit the truth to Mademoiselle Simonette would bring only anger and scorn upon her head.

'Well?' Simonette demanded. 'I await an explanation. Your father requires of me a complete account of all your doings.'

Mary hovered on one foot uncertainly, all the joy of the afternoon fading swiftly under Simonette's accusing glare. From the corner of her eye she was aware of Anne's listening figure in the shadows of the passage.

'I — I have been walking by the stream, down to the village,' she murmured in confusion. Anne's dark eyes brightened with interest and she moved closer to listen.

'To the village?' Simonette echoed in amazement. 'Alone, unescorted? What were you thinking of pray? And what would your father say if he knew?'

She turned about, taking hold of Mary's arm firmly and drawing her towards the bedchamber. While she watched Mary pulling off her faded gown her face registered disapproval, grimacing with cold disgust.

'You spoke to none of the villagers, I hope?' she questioned icily, the thick scorn in her voice implying that answer was unnecessary as no well-nurtured maid would dream of doing aught so demeaning. Her glittering eyes widened sharply at Mary's answer.

'Only to a youth who was cutting the grass.'

Anne leapt forward eagerly out of the shadows to pull Mary by the hand to face her. 'Tell us, oh tell us Mary! Did you coquette with him? Was it fun, or was he stupid and doltish?'

Before Mary could protest Simonette caught Anne by the shoulder and turned her briskly about. 'Enough mistress Anne. Be good enough to leave us alone.'

Anne's bright eyes clouded with disappointment, and she dawdled as she went, anxious, no doubt, to hear more of her sister's exploit. But Simonette closed the door firmly behind her and came back to face Mary, her back straight and stiff and her hands folded neatly before her. Piece by piece she dragged from her charge the details of the afternoon's outing, her face set grimly as she listened.

'So, you cavorted shamelessly in the grass with this lout, with not a thought for your family's pride,' she muttered through clenched teeth when Mary had done.

'He is no lout, Simonette; he is gentle and kind!' Mary protested, her voice shrill with dismay.

'With no thought for your family,' Simonette reiterated. 'Nor for the possible consequences.'

'Consequences?' Mary echoed faintly.

Simonette's sigh was one of exhausted patience, not of sadness. 'Indeed, Mistress Mary. The consequences of such wanton behaviour could well have been a bastard child, and you are not so simple that you did not know it. Do you think your father would let you marry a common village lad, and you an Earl's granddaughter? Had you no thought for the shame you would bring him?'

Mary stared at her infuriated eyes, glittering back with scorn, and felt helpless and afraid and at the same time angry. There had been no wicked thought in her mind as she lay in the grass, welcoming Rafe's caresses, and Simonette was cruel to believe it. The governess paced the chamber in agitation.

'I would never have believed it! Granted, you are no

scholar, but I did not take you for a simpleton either! Hurling yourself at a youth with such abandon, inviting his embrace!! She swung round furiously on her charge, standing now barefoot and nearly naked before her. 'Like a bitch on heat — *c'est incroyable* — but it is in the blood. Mistress, you do not leave the castle again until I have orders from your father, you understand?'

Nodding miserably, Mary went to bathe her burning face in the cool water in the ewer and heard the door slam after Simonette's angry exit. Poor Simonette. It was years of frustrated spinsterhood that made her speak with such venom, Mary thought sadly, but her animal analogy cast a filthy slime over Mary's friendship with Rafe nonetheless. It was only as Mary lay on the bed, tearfully indignant at Simonette's ugly imputations, which implied that her meeting with Rafe was in some way disgusting and dishonourable, that Anne crept into the chamber. She climbed eagerly on to the bed.

'Tell me about it, Mall. Was it exciting?'

Mary rolled over, burying her hot face in the cool pillow.

'Oh *do* tell me, Mall. I'm longing to know what it's like to be seduced.'

Mary turned tear-filled eyes angrily on her sister. 'I was *not* seduced. We did no wrong, Rafe and I — it was innocent, it was loving and gentle — and so beautiful.'

And would have been more beautiful yet if they had not been interrupted. But it was doubly cruel to be unjustly accused of what she had not savoured. Mary wept noisily, and Anne's slender fingers slid out to stroke her trembling shoulders.

'Do not weep, Mall. Perchance Simonette will not tell Father after all, for he will be sorely angered with her for letting you slip away. She will not risk his displeasure unnecessarily. So dry your eyes. With luck you will not be punished after all.'

Mary wept the louder, but it was not so much fear of Sir

Thomas's anger that caused the tears to flood, as the realisation that now she would never be able to see Rafe again. Sinomette's eagle eye would see to that.

The governess's swiftly-despatched letter brought in reply, not a sealed letter of orders, but Sir Thomas himself, thundering into the castle courtyard on horseback, his face dark with anger. Flinging the reins of his horse to an apprehensive ostler, he strode swiftly into the castle, his clattering spurs denoting the extent of his ire. Mary was summoned peremptorily to his presence. Simonette stood, eyes downcast and hands demurely folded as, Sir Thomas paced the chamber, still cloaked and cracking his riding crop angrily against his thigh as he walked.

'What is this I hear, mistress?' he hissed menacingly as Mary entered and made her obeisance. 'You, of noble blood, letting yourself be tumbled by village lads! How dare you face me so, daughter, meek-faced and all innocence in your eyes when you have dared to betray me thus! Do you seek to cozen me, your father, with your guileless looks? Do you think I would look away while you tarnish our name and bear me bastard grandchildren? No! Do not seek to answer me, you wanton, or I fear lest I put my whip to work about you. But do not think to dissemble further, mistress, for I have the measure of you now. I do not propose to let all my concern and expense for your education be wasted, for I have better plans for you and your sister.'

He paused to let his words take effect, his normally pale face still flushed with unspent anger. Mary knew better than to attempt to explain, for Sir Thomas was a man to whom silent acceptance was essential. To reply, however meekly, would be tantamount to insolence in his eyes, and the beating he threatened would undoubtedly become fact.

Sir Thomas cleared his throat. 'Get you hence to your chamber, mistress, and have your tiring-women begin to pack your belongings and those of your sister too.' He turned to Simonette. 'Mademoiselle, have all ready to depart for Blickling in the morning.'

Simonette bobbed a curtsey and withdrew. Mary stood aghast. For her crimes, real or not, she and Anne were to be banished to the quietude of Norfolk, out of reach of amorous village swains. And it was deeply hurtful to know her father believed her cheap and stupid. Sir Thomas dismissed her with an angry wave, as if unwilling to spend more scornful words on her. Mary withdrew meekly.

Wistfully she began the preparations for the journey, saddened at the prospect of not feeling Rafe's warm arms ing Blickling and busying herself eagerly with supervising her packing, was nonetheless curious.
vising her packing, was nonetheless curious.

'Was Father very angry, Mall? Did you really lie with your swain? Do you love him, Mall?'

Mary shook her golden curls slowly. 'He was not my lover, Anne, but I welcomed his friendship.'

'You should have been more discreet, had a ready tale to tell Simonette to conceal your meetings,' said Anne easily. 'You are too simple, Mary, too trusting and honest. Next time I shall help you devise a plan.'

Her slanting dark eyes registered innocent sympathy, but Mary was shocked nonetheless. For all her youth Anne was far more world-wise and scheming than Mary could ever be. Mother had been right. This child would carve her own career in the world without the help of anyone. Still, Anne's words held out a promise — there would be other occasions for Mary to enjoy friendship and warmth, and next time she would indeed be more careful.

Hemp-bound boxes carried their belongings to Blickling the following day, and when she saw the stately mansion set among magnificent old oak and chestnut trees drawing into sight Mary felt no longer dispirited. Optimism flooded her veins. An air of promise and expectancy lay over the lush Norfolk countryside as they threaded their way along the green aisles of the park.

In the succeeding weeks Sir Thomas spoke no more of the incident which had excited his wrath, but his taciturn, behaviour and unexplained excursions from the hall indicated that he had little wish to communicate with his errant daughter. When at last he had news to impart, he did so with typical abruptness.

'George will be home next week,' he announced and as Mary's and Anne's faces both brightened with expectation he continued, 'to attend my wedding. Then you shall meet your new stepmother, Lady Beth.'

CHAPTER FOUR

PRELUDE

IN the privacy of the solar the two girls bent over their needlework, discussing the significance of their father's startling announcement.

'I wonder at his decision,' commented Mary thoughtfully. 'Our beloved mother dead barely two years and he thinks to re-marry.'

Anne smiled knowingly as she selected another thread for her needle. 'It is not so surprising, Mall, for our father knows what he is about. He has need of a mother for his children, a housekeeper who will not drain his purse, so he selects a countrywoman of simple tastes. She will not demand court dresses nor jewellery, but being of yeoman stock. She will keep house thriftily and be a responsible guardian for Father's wayward children. Simonette did her best but she had no paternal jurisdiction over us and as Father is so often away at Court, Lady Beth will rule us in his stead. It is a simple, economical expedient for Father to re-marry.'

Mary turned her sister's words over in her mind. From what Sir Thomas had told them of his future wife it would seem Anne was right, but what manner of woman would this stepmother be? One thing was certain; she could never be so beautiful and admired and coveted as Lady Elizabeth had been, nor perhaps as kindly. Mary ventured the thought to Anne, who laughed.

'She is no doubt a dragon of a woman, thin and sharp and shrill-voiced, just as stepmothers always are in fairy tales. But I shall take no heed of her save only outwardly.

Deep down inside I shall think my own thoughts and do as I please, and I counsel you to do likewise, Mall, and not fret for our own mother.'

Making no answer, Mary stitched on. It was all very well for Anne in her closeness with Tom Wyatt to plan to ignore their stepmother, for Tom's father Sir Henry had now moved his family close by, in order to see to his duties at Norwich Castle. But for Mary there was no one, only the advent of this new parent to enliven her days. She waited apprehensively for the bride's arrival, for, unlike Anne she could not regard the prospect with equanimity, aloof and disdainful. Vulnerable and timid as she was, the newcomer could bruise her already sensitive heart yet more deeply.

Then suddenly, the new mistress of Blickling Hall was there, short and plump and her gown decidedly dowdy, but there was no doubting the honesty and warmth that glowed in her genial brown eyes. Her arms outstretched to welcome her stepchildren with cries of joy, she seemed so homely and her embrace so genuine that Mary's diffidence dissolved instantaneously. Anne and George, though courteous in their greeting, were less responsive than Mary, and she could see the judicious contemplation in their dark eyes and the resolve to withhold judgement until they had bettered their acquaintance with their new mother. To George the matter was of little interest in any event, for he would soon be returning to the vivid life of London and the Court.

Anne's manner towards the new lady mistress of the house remained determinedly cool despite Lady Beth's uncalculating warmth and the ambience of maternal feeling, and it was only after Sir Thomas had left Blickling for Court abruptly, exhortations to wife and daughters completed, that Anne's manner began to soften. Mary was pleased, for she had given her heart unreservedly to the gentle-eyed woman with the low, slow-spoken Norfolk accent.

'You *do* like Lady Beth, don't you, Anne?'

Anne shrugged non-committally. 'She is kindly and well-meaning, I fancy, and she certainly does not harass us over an idle spinning-wheel or unopened books as Father does. I think mayhap I shall grow fond of her in time, and then I shall not miss George so sorely.'

She spoke less than the truth, for in the months to come Mary discovered a growing closeness between her sister and stepmother, and once again she feared lest Anne's brilliance should outshine her completely. But there she underestimated Lady Beth, for with diplomatic affection the older woman shared her attentive ear and maternal solicitude between the two girls equally. Anne's resistance was completely crumbled; now instead she sought to please her stepmother, to delight her with a surprise nosegay of wild flowers or the ripest quince from the orchard, and Mary began to savour again the peace of domestic intimacy and love that she had lacked for so long. For the time being there was no further need of succouring masculine arms to soothe and delight as Rafe's had done, and contentment rested like a warm blanket over Blickling during that winter.

Spring, 1514, was mercifully mild and full of promise. Sir Thomas, now busier than ever serving his master the King since he had been appointed Ambassador to France, came home less and less frequently and would have been sorely disappointed to know how little he was missed by his family. They were all safely ensconced once more at Hever when word came of Sir Thomas's imminent arrival for a brief visit.

Buds were burgeoning on the tall trees surrounding the castle as Mary watched from a high latticed window for her father's arrival and she felt a vague sense of disquiet. It was as though with the rising of the sap, there was a birth of new, unknown emotions within her young breast. It was a tenuous, shifting longing for something intangible, a yearning for freedom and vehement sensations. Mary shivered at the strange emotion, but then suddenly Father's huge dominating presence filled the castle, his whiplike voice demanding and peremptory, and the feeling faded.

Having eaten and refreshed himself, Sir Thomas bid Lady Beth stop fussing over him and send his daughters to him in the study. He sat with furrowed brow behind his vast oak desk, deep in concentration on the papers in his hand as Mary and Anne entered, curtseyed and stood waiting in respectful silence. Simonette stood with bowed head behind them and awaited the inevitable barked demands as to their progress.

But they did not come. Instead Sir Thomas cleared his throat and leaned forward over his desk, surveying his daughters critically before speaking.

'My children, as you know, as a trusted servant of His Grace the King I am entrusted with many important matters on his behalf.' He paused, as if expecting an acknowledgment of his position of consequence in His Majesty's Court, but meeting only expectant silence, he continued. 'This year, as Ambassador to France, the most earnest matter of the Princess Mary Rose's forthcoming marriage to King Louis of France has been confided to my capable hands, and I am proud of the honour His Grace confers upon me.'

Arching his fingertips together Sir Thomas permitted himself a thin-lipped smile of contentment. Anne, wide-eyed, could not resist exclaiming, 'The princess is to wed an old man? Oh, it is monstrous, Papa!'

Sir Thomas frowned. 'Hold your tongue, girl! The Princess is sixteen, a woman grown, and King Louis is but fifty-three, and is like to have many years before him yet. In any event the marriage is politically necessary, to ensure peace between England and France in these turbulent days, but let me continue. The Princess will, of course, have need of her own train of ladies-in-waiting to accompany her to the French Court in September. Already three have been chosen — the Ladies Anne and Elizabeth Grey, and the youngest daughter of Lord Dacres. One place remained to be filled and, as I have the King's ear, I considered it might be a highly expedient move to suggest my daughter, thus acquiring for her an education she might not otherwise attain.'

Three pairs of eyes fastened expectantly on Sir Thomas's stern face. In the bosoms of the two girls hope leapt, each burning with curiosity to know which daughter Sir Thomas had selected, but he was not anxious to relinquish his moment of power.

'Simonette,' he addressed the pale-faced governess severely, 'How well does each of my daughters speak French?'

Simonette hesitated, nervously pleating a fold of her sombre kirtle. 'Mistress Anne speaks and writes the language fluently, Sir Thomas, though not without flaw.'

'And Mary?'

'Mistress Mary's French is passable.'

Hope receded in Mary's breast. Convicted by faint praise, she would undoubtedly be passed over now for the gleaming promise of a life as lady-in-waiting to the new Queen of France. To Anne would go the glory and the vivid life at the French Court. She hung her head shame-facedly, wishing, too late now, that she had tried harder to learn and become clever like Anne. At fifteen, to be superseded by a sister younger by two years was shameful.

'I see.' Sir Thomas reflected for a moment, then dipped his quill pen in the ink-horn and scratched busily for some minutes, while the silence hung heavy with apprehension in the book-lined study. At last he put down the quill.

'There, now it is done. Mary, as the elder, shall accompany the Princess in her train. But wait,' he added, seeing Anne's crestfallen look. 'there is more. As you are nearing thirteen, Anne, you too could well profit from a sojourn in France, and to that end I have written to my kinsman, the Comte de Brie, to ask him to take you into his household. If he agrees, as I am certain he will, you shall travel with Mary in September. It behoves you both to behave with the dignity and decorum that is fitting to your station.'

Neither girl listened to Sir Thomas's prolonged exhortation as to their conduct in France. Each was living in a private daydream, a longing to begin the life this sudden news unfolded before them.

Mary was ecstatic. It was as if a miraculous answer had been granted to her yearning of the morning; the only blemish was that she hoped Anne was not too disappointed.

'Not I!' cried Anne, swirling round and round in their bedchamber in uncontrollable delight. 'New gowns — just think of it, Mall! A whole new wardrobe of gowns and cloaks and shoes, when usually Papa makes us lengthen and unpick all our old gowns! And I am to live as a guest in the château of a real comte, just like a titled lady! Oh Mall! We shall become so fine, so honoured and sought-after when we return! I can hardly wait for September!'

The feverish activity in preparation for their departure lasted throughout the summer and the only saddened heart at Hever was that of Lady Beth, dismayed at the coming loss of her two remaining stepchildren.

'You will take care now, won't you, Mary?' Her lips trembled anxiously as she considered the plight of the gentle, vulnerable child. 'They say the French are wicked people, given to much drinking and debauching, and I fear for your safety.'

'Not for Anne's?' Mary replied. 'She is younger than I.'

'She has Simonette to accompany and chaperone her; you have no one. Yet I should trust our good Princess to have a care to her ladies, for she has grown up at Queen Catherine's court and by all accounts our Queen is a devoutly religious lady. Yes, for sure the Princess will see to it that her ladies behave in a fitting God-fearing manner and that no harm befalls them.'

Thus assured, Lady Beth busied herself in the many preparations. The Comte de Brie wrote to exclaim how delighted he would be to entertain Mistress Anne and to help further her studies, and Sir Thomas was content with his well-conceived plans. Now he would not only acquire a good education for his daughters abroad, but at the same time he would spare his own pocket the expenses of their upbringing for the next few years. It was a comfortable position to hold, that of the King's Ambassador, and with careful foresight and diligence Sir Thomas might expect to add to his honours — nay, a title even — before long. In the meantime he must see to it that his daughters were well-disciplined in the arts of court-curtseying, and the intricate protocol of the nobility, for they must bring him credit when they came under Royal eyes.

Mary was the first to be displayed. As attendant to the Princess it behoved her to attend the Princess's proxy marriage to be held at Greenwich in August, and as Sir Thomas rode to London with his elder daughter by his side, he surveyed her critically. She was pale, frightened no doubt, but she was undoubtedly a beauty and carried herself with natural grace. It was a pity she was so docile and slow in comparison with Anne, who with her quick wits and Boleyn shrewdness would have known instinctively how best to profit from such a situation. Confidante to Mary Rose, sister of England's King and wife to the French King, was infinitely more suitable for Anne than this cow-like Mary here, but it would have been unseemly to show preference for the younger child. Never mind, there was still time to arrange Anne's introduction to the French court when the monemt was ripe. In the meantime Mary's fragile beauty, gold and glistening like a summer rose, was sure to catch some eminent eye and it would be a further feather in Thomas's cap if she acquired herself a titled Frenchman to husband.

No eventuality escaped Sir Thomas's ranging mind. There was just a flicker of doubt about Mary's possible corruption at the French court, for he remembered still the incident of the village lad — it had come to naught, of course but with Mary's gullible nature it might well have done. There was a trace of the flibbertigibbet about her, a hint of the flightiness that had rendered his first wife so desirable to all men. He must remember to speak to Mary once again before the time came to embark at Dover.

It was a hot, still August day and the church of the Grey Friars in Greenwich was crowded. Mary was so bedazzled by the myriad multi-hued gowns and robes of the courtiers that she could scarcely register the principal actors in the scene before her — her new mistress the slender, pallid Princess Mary Rose, the handsome young proxy bridegroom the Duc de Longueville — and most magnetic of them all, the tall, golden figure of the King, young Henry of England.

It seemed almost inconceivable that this young lion of England, broad of shoulder, with shining eyes, with red-gold hair glinting in the shafts of sunlight, handsome beyond compare in his richly-jewelled doublet, should be husband to the dumpy, thickening Queen Catherine who sat stolid and impassive beside him. He was tall and vibrant, towering above his courtiers, impressively athletic and god-like in his bearing, yet she was diminutive, her face already ageing and tired.

How ill-matched they seemed, thought Mary, and instantly repented of the unkind thought. The poor Queen was already nearing thirty, seven years older than her husband, and it was but recently she had lost her third son in her constant attempts to provide Henry with an heir. It was rumoured she was already pregnant again, and judging from her haggard appearance and squat body, Mary judged it was highly likely.

Sir Thomas interrupted Mary's thoughts to nudge her and whisper, 'Remember after the ceremony to address the Princess no longer as Highness but as Majesty, for she is now Queen of France.'

Mary nodded. So much to remember, so much to try to register and learn, and when they eventually reached France, no doubt there would be much more to learn again. It was consoling, however, that her new mistress appeared so warm and human despite her royal blood. She scrutinised Mary Rose's pretty face, spectre-like in its pallor in the shadows of the church. She appeared outwardly calm and composed, but Mary recalled the reddened eyes the Princess had inadvertently revealed to her before they had left Placentia, the King's palace at Greenwich. Instinctively Mary could sense there was sorrow behind the Princess's wedding finery and she felt an immediate bond of sympathy with the maid only a year older than herself.

The secret of Mary Rose's sorrow was no secret but open gossip, Sir Thomas told his daughter when she commented upon the fact later.

'It is common knowledge that the Princess — Her Majesty — has given her heart unwisely to Charles Brandon, the Duke of Suffolk, before she learned of His Majesty's plans for her and King Louis. Mary Rose only gave way to the King at last and acceded to his demand on condition that if and when she re-marries, it may be to a man of her own choosing, Which,' added Sir Thomas, stroking his beard thoughtfully, 'may be nearer than His Majesty realises, for I have intelligence that Louis of France is already sickly and has to arrange his life just as his physicians order if he hopes to prolong it.'

Mary was horrified. To think that the peach-skinned maid, so pale and composed, was doomed to surrender her charms to a feeble, ailing old man to aid her country's cause! Already, though she barely knew her mistress, Mary felt her concern and sympathy for the girl blossom and flourish.

The time was come. The baggage, including Mary's own chests full of richly-trimmed gowns of velvet and brocade, were loaded on to carts and pack horses and transported to Dover for the Royal bride's embarkation to meet her husband. As if in sympathy for the reluctant young wife the weather stormed for a whole month, tempests raging along the coast so that the only ships that ventured to put to sea were instantly wrecked and their crews drowned. Mary sat patiently with her silent, uncomplaining mistress and wondered, a little apprehensively, yet with a certain amount of excitement, what the unknown life ahead would bring.

CHAPTER FIVE

SCHERZO

IT was October before the storms abated sufficiently for the royal bride to set sail for France, and during that time King Henry entertained his favourite sister in Dover Castle. During that time the wonder-filled eyes of the Princess's young lady-in-waiting, Mary Boleyn, had ample time to gaze upon and admire the magnificence of England's youthful King, handsome beyond compare both in dress and in person. And on one occasion he even spoke to her, a light of pleasure dawning in his eyes as his gaze fell upon her.

'Ah, my sister's pretty little maid. How are you named, mistress?', he asked warmly, dallying a moment in one of the passages in the castle and causing his companions to wait and watch.

'Mary Boleyn, Your Grace,' Mary dropped a low curtsey, her cheeks suffused with pleasure at such royal favour. Henry extended a slim hand, heavily be-ringed.

'Ah yes, my trusted Sir Thomas's child. Rise, mistress Mary. I pray you have a good care to your mistress on her journey,' His voice, resonant and low, made Mary dizzy with delight.

'Rest assured, Sire, I shall,' she replied softly, eyes downcast. Henry nodded and strolled on to rejoin his companions.

It was still not yet dawn when one morning Henry accompanied the Princess Mary Rose to the beach to watch her departure.

Sir Thomas Boleyn felt his agitation of the past month

begin to lessen gradually as he watched the King's tender farewell embrace of his sister but he knew he would not be truly content until he had safely accomplished his mission to hand over the new French Queen to her ageing, impatient husband. Nevertheless, he looked away discreetly on seeing the tears glisten in Mary Rose's eyes as she looked up at her tall young brother for perhaps the last time, and he talked gruffly instead with the Duke of Norfolk and the Earl of Surrey.

Leaden skies lowered ominously as the coast of England faded from view in the dawn light, and before long the rains lashed and the winds howled once more. During the crossing Thomas saw naught of the French Queen, locked away in her cabin with her ladies, but perhaps that was as well, he reflected, for to see his daughter Mary white-faced and ill as most were during the storm, would have rendered him equally queasy. Occasionally he caught a glimpse of Anne on deck, cloaked and hooded and pointing out excitedly the grey-green walls of sea to a very disinterested Simonette. His duties would not be completed until he had delivered Mary Rose to Abbeville and, thereafter, Anne and Simonette to Brie. By then King Henry would be anxiously awaiting his return to hear a detailed account of Mary Rose's grand ceremonial wedding.

For Mistress Mary Boleyn the Channel crossing was dismal, her royal mistress remaining silent and brooding and the other ladies-in-waiting being too pre-occupied with sea-sickness to offer to converse. It was with a tremendous feeling of relief that she heard at last that Boulogne was in sight. The boat which carried her and the hollow-eyed Princess ashore rocked perilously, but once safely ashore the discomforts of the journey were soon forgotten. A vast and distinguished company of French nobles headed by Francis, Duke of Angoulême, all eager to see their new Queen, waited on the quay, Anne nudged Mary.

'Tis a pity our Princess looks so bedraggled after the

journey, but I'll warrant her beauty conquers them none-theless.'

With all pomp and splendour the travellers were escort-ed by the young Duke into the town. Mary's ears were assail-ed on all sides by rapid French conversation, of which she could make out little, but Anne replied brightly and with fluent charm. After rest and a welcome meal, the journey proceeded. Sir Thomas bustled about anxiously to ensure, that the ladies were comfortable in their litters or mount-ed on palfreys which befitted their station, and Mary could not resist a thrill of delight on seeing the Princess's pal-frey, beautifully caparisoned in cloth of gold. King Louis evidently intended well for his new bride, for Duke Francis announced that he had also sent magnificent gowns of crimson velvet for her ladies. Mary flushed with plea-sure, especially when she saw her father's approving con-sideration of her sister and herself.

And Duke Francis's smile showed he, too, found her appearance pleasing. He was comely, this young Duke, much of an age with King Henry and not unlike him with his broad-shouldered height and dark-gold hair, and almost as handsome but for his somewhat long nose. And there was that in his langurous smile which betokened the same sup-pressed virility, she thought with a shiver.

They reached Abbeville at last, and Mary's spitirs soared. Masques and music accompanied the royal entry into the town, Duke Francis beaming proudly as he rode, but the beautiful young bride looked more downcast than ever. Here they were to meet the royal bridegroom. Excitedly he rode into the town, the aged King, elegantly adorned to match the Princess's finery and mounted on a capricious Spanish mare which threw his old body about like a boneless floursack. When Mary saw the stooping, shuffling old man who dismounted to clutch feverishly at Mary Rose's hand, she could well understand her mistress's misery. To be forced to abjure a younger, more handsome man like

Brandon in order to be wived to this senile, wizened creature called for great self-denial and loyalty to her brother. Even though Mary knew her mistress but little yet, she had given her all her respect and admiration. Life at the French Court would not be all sunshine and merriment with this reluctant, sad-faced Queen to serve, but with the passing of time she might grow brighter.

But more hardship was yet to befall the young Princess. In order to have his Queen more exclusively to himself, King Louis ordered that her ladies leave and return to England forthwith. Mary Rose looked aghast.

'Even my old nurse, Mother Guildford?' she exclaimed.

'All, all,' the old King's treble shrilled. 'But stay — one may remain, just one lady of your choice. But the rest must leave at once.'

Even the lavish ball that night, ordered by Duke Francis, did little to erase the sadness from Mary Rose's pretty piquant face. Next day all her ladies were gone, save Mistress Mary Boleyn.

'You I shall keep, Mary,' she murmured softly as Mary brushed her long hair. 'You, because we are much of an age, you and I.'

And Mary read her meaning, that their mutual youth and innocence would give them a bond of sympathy that not even a lifelong nurse could share.

On the morning after the Royal wedding Sir Thomas came to bid farewell to Mary.

'After delivering your sister Anne to Brie I must hasten back to Greenwich,' he told her briskly. 'But before I leave, let me remind you once again of my former admonition. These French courtiers seem given to over-much levity and coquetry and I know the extent of your impressionable nature. Have a care, therefore, that you let no blemish attach to our respected name.'

Mary smiled, that sweet, ingenuous smile that reminded him so much of her mother. 'Have no fear, Father. I shall tend my mistress well and reflect only credit to our name, for she has my sympathy utterly.'

Sir Thomas snorted. Such sentimental rubbish women talked! Sympathy indeed! The Princess had done well to become Queen of France instead of only Duchess of Suffolk if she'd had her way. He regarded Mary's composed, grave little face thoughtfully. Perhaps he had no need to say more. The wench was slow and gave her affections easily, but if it were Mary Rose she sentimentalised over, so much the better, far better than green love-sickness over some youth.

'Your sister waits to bid you farewell,' he said curtly, and bending to kiss Mary quickly on the cheek, he turned and strode from the chamber. Within seconds the door opened again and Anne, already cloaked and hooded for the journey, entered with a smile.

Her slanting eyes flashed merrily as she took Mary's hands in hers. 'So now we must leave you to enjoy the gaiety and glamour of court life, unchaperoned. How lucky you are, Mary, for I shall be under Simonette's hawk-eyed surveillance! How quiet it will be, deep in the country and immersed in study, far removed from you and Court.'

Mary squeezed her hands. 'You will do well, Anne, as you always do, and Father will be proud of you. Do not fret, though I confess I shall miss you sorely.'

'Then neither do you fret, Mall, for I swear I shall not miss you for long.' The green twinkle flashed all the brighter. Mary looked at her, mystified.

'What do you mean, Anne?'

Anne's chuckle was low but laughter-filled. 'I promise you this, Mall, you will not be without me for long, for as soon as I may I shall follow you to the French Court. When my studies are done and I have eaten heartily of French food till I am plump and shapely, then I shall come. See how thin I am now?' She threw back the cloak to reveal her boyish, flat-breasted figure, swirled about, then grasped Mary's hands again. 'When I have grown me a bosom and buttocks, Mall, then I shall return, I swear it, or my name is not Anne Boleyn!'

Sir Thomas knocked sharply and re-entered.

'Come, Anne, 'tis time.'

Tears escaped Mary's eyes as she sat in a window embrasure and watched her father ride off, the waving figure of Anne riding behind him. Now there was no one from home, nothing familiar to cling to and treasure, only the young, fragile Mary Rose.

Within days Mary realised how wrong she was. Mary Rose, far from being fragile and chastened, suddenly appeared, to jerk into life, like a puppet at the end of some unseen string. All sullenness dropped from her like some unwanted mantle and she flung herself into energetic activity. Louis, delighted that his listless wife seemed suddenly to have revived, entered her every plan with eager alacrity.

'A hunt today I think, Louis my dear,' the tall, slender bride would announce brightly, and Mary watched with some amusement as poor King Louis was hoisted by his menservants to mount a lively horse while Mary Rose waited impatiently, her mount already frisking to be away. And when Mary Rose returned from the hunt, eyes ashine and cheeks whipped into colour from the frenzy of the chase, it was not to rest and recover but to call Mistress Boleyn to help her change her costume ready to begin dancing.

'Come, play me the lute, Mary, while I practise the steps of these new French dances,' the young Queen would command, and by night she led the court dancing proudly, drawing her dear Louis to his feet again whenever he begged to sit and recover his breath. Mary Rose would have none of it and poor Louis, anxious to please the wife once so lacklustre and sad but now miraculously indefatigable, complied willingly.

Mary felt sorry for the old King and could not understand the sudden change in her mistress, but as Mary Rose
offered no explanation, it remained a mystery. Louis'
courtiers, however, regarded the situation both with amusement and disapprobation.

But there had never been a time like it in her life before,
Mary reflected contentedly. All round her now there was
life and gaiety, rumour and intrigue and spicy snippets of
gossip to be learnt from the other ladies in the mess hall
as they sat over supper. Her ears gradually acclimatising
to their swiftly-spoken French, Mary became intrigued by
what she overheard.

'I see Duke Francis comes to Court more often now the
new Queen has enlivened the place.'

'Ah, trust Francis Foxnose to be where fun and beautiful
women are to be found.'

'A pity he chose such a plain, dumpy wife as Claude
then, if he admires the beauties so.'

'There his mother, Louise of Savoy, knew what she was
about. Claude may be no beauty but she is King Louis's
heir, so long as the new Queen bears him no son. With
Claude our Foxnose will inherit the throne when Louis
dies.'

'Then poor Francis' nose will be put out of joint if
Mary Rose provides Louis with a son. So much for his
mother's plans then.'

Shrieks of hilarity met this remark. 'Think you our
poor King has a chance of having a child! So much dancing
and kissing-in-the-ring, he is worn out long before he
goes to bed! No, *mon amie*, the throne is safe for Francis
and Claude.'

Mary had no need to ask to whom they referred, for the
sobriquet Foxnose indicated only too well the tall young
Duke Francis of the fox-red hair who smiled indulgently
at all Louis' capers and ogled every pretty wench within

arm's reach. She had seen him almost every night in the ballroom when she escorted her mistress, with his indolent smile and a caressing look that sent delicious shivers up one's spine. Even among the numerous courtiers elegantly clad and bejewelled the young Duke's athlecit figure in its magnificent costume stood out, regal and commanding. Not unlike, thought Mary once again with a tremor, the handsome, imposing presence of King Henry. Once more she remembered how, watching from under lowered lashes, she had seen Henry tenderly embrace his sister in farewell, the girl leaning against his broad, protective shoulder and how he had smiled favourably upon her too.

Duke Francis had the same power of arousing interest among the ladies of the French Court. Mary was not blind to the coquettish, downcast glances and pert looks he received from the ladies, and neither was he. His deep-set blue eyes gleamed with mischievous fire in answer to the coy glances darted his way, and when Mary felt his appraising gaze rest briefly on her, she felt uncomfortably gauche and at the same time, fascinated by the man. French courtiers were so gay, so frivolous and sophisticated that she felt extremely ill-at-ease and unable to compete.

But by degrees receiving compliments gracefully became less harassing and more delighting to Mary's easily-responsive nature. It was pleasant to be praised for one's sensitive playing of the rebec or for one's melodious voice, instead of receiving only harsh criticism and exhortations to try harder as she had at the hands of Simonette and her father. Blossoming in the warmth of approval, Mary felt happier than she had ever done before. The gentlemen were ever attentive and courteous to her, and by night, when the servants lit the numerous candles, sly caresses and surreptitious kisses in deserted corners made Mary glow with contentment. She might not have Anne's cleverness to compete in witty French conversation, but some of the polish of suave manners and refinement was gradually attaching to her behaviour, and she was evidently admired and pursued.

Her mistress, Mary Rose, busily occupied with her own hectic life, noticed little of what her lady-in-waiting did, but on one occasion as Mary braided the young Queen's hair she did venture to advise her.

'I hope you are enjoying the attentions of the many handsome, cultured young men about the court, Mary.'

'Indeed, Madame.'

'Have a care only with that lusty Duke Francis, my dear, for I hear he has bedded every pretty wench about the Court. His poor wife, heavy with child as she is and plain into the bargain, must find him a terrible trial. I would not wish him to get my ladies with child.'

'Have no fear, Madame.' But the Queen's words had thrilled Mary. Francis was immensely attractive, lean and virile, and his glances had shown he found Mary lissom and lovely too. Mentally Mary savoured a caress from the slim fingered hand and shivered with pleasure. But for the time being clandestine embraces in a curtained alcove or in a terrace arbour with other court gallants kept Mary's senses alive and joyful. It was so flattering to see ardent young men abandoning other court beauties in order to pursue her, Mary Boleyn, despite all her lack of finesse and ignorance of sophisticated coquetry. To amend any appearance of being a country bumpkin, Mary studied their dress and mannerisms carefully and emulated them as best she could. Still covetous male eyes followed her as well as jealous female ones.

It was one winter evening as Mary hastened along a deserted, draughty corridor of the palace to fetch rosewater for Her Majesty's toilet that she made closer acquaintance with Francis of the fox-brush hair.

She might have turned the corner without noticing the tall figure shrouded in the wainscoted shadows, but he stepped forward as he passed, making Mary catch her breath in alarm. Strong, slender fingers caught her elbow. 'Mademoiselle, I beg you, take no fright. Rather let me apologise for alarming so fair a maid.'

Mary fluttered, clutching the precious phial to her bosom. 'I did not know someone stood in the shadows; I was taken by surprise, that is all.'

'Would that you were, mademoiselle.' She did not follow his meaning, but she saw clearly the gleam of humour in his eyes. 'You are one of Madame la Reine's little English roses, are you not? How are you named?' The voice, deep and resonant, was music to Mary's ears.

'Mary Boleyn, sir.'

'Marie Boullan,' he repeated, and his Gallic pronunciation of her name, a thing so very personal, sounded deliciously attractive. 'Will you not come and sit with me, Mademoiselle Marie, here on the window seat?' He waved graciously with one hand, indicating a cushioned seat in the mullioned window, and took Mary's elbow encouraging with the other. Mary hesitated. She should be about her business, but Duke Francis was not only handsome and courteous, but he had also that intangible air of animal delight in the senses that one possessor instantly recognises in another. Mary was reluctant to leave this magnetic man, this dark, deserted gallery.

'Her Majesty awaits her rose-water,' she pleaded shyly and Francis, recognising the reluctance to leave, laughed softly, the pressure on her elbow becoming more insistent.

'Then Madame should not send her fairest English flower on such an errand if she hopes to see the maid again. She should be sufficiently familiar with a Frenchman's keen eye for beauty by now to know that, like the bee, he will endeavour to savour the nectar of such a rose. Such a rose,' he repeated softly, drawing Mary down on to the seat, 'so creamy and petal-smooth is your skin.' His tapered fingers rested lightly on the low cut front of her bodice, caressing the contours of her breast. Mary shivered with delicious anticipation. His fingers, softer and more tender than Rafe's had ever been, aroused a storm of feeling in her that clamoured for expression. She sat, passive and wide-eyed and yearning for more. The phial was clutched tightly between her hands.

'So fragrant, so wholesome and unblemished,' he was murmuring, his face, indistinct in the half light looming closer to her own. His lips brushed hers. 'Such honeyed breath, luring the bee to venture further,' said the mellifluous voice, while the silken fingers probed. Mary melted against him, her flesh eager and her limbs weak with desire. Like an expert lyrist he knew how to handle an instrument with such delicacy and finesse that he drew every ounce of feeling from it, and Mary was a willing instrument to such a man. The world about her dimmed in a haze of ecstasy. The phial slipped from her trembling fingers and shattered sending a heady scent of summer-crushed rose petals to invade her nostrils, intoxicating, sensual and tormenting.

'A veritable rose, ripe for the plucking,' Francis' hoarse voice murmured in her ear.

CHAPTER SIX

TOCCATA

IT really was too thoughtless of the Queen, enchanting as she was, to choose that very moment to send another of her laides in quest of the rose-water and thus intrude upon the wonderful dream Mary and Francis were about to share. Mary was enclosed in his arms, hovering on the dizzying brink of a profounder ecstasy into which she was longing to plunge, when the voice, rude and uninvited, shattered the fantasy into a million slivers. She could have wept with frustration.

Francis was furious. He watched the two figures retreating down the passage, his gaze fixed lustfully on the plump buttocks of the little English maid, trying to master the pumping beat in his loins that screamed for those silken thighs he had caressed under their covering of velvet. It was too vexing! She had been all pliant and willing, her flesh leaping to his touch in a way that held out infinite promise. The rose had nearly been his, and his brain was still benumbed by her heady perfume.

Miserably he kicked the broken phial at his feet. The maid *must* be his, on that he was determined, and Duke Francis was seldom unable to attain that which he desired. There was something so indefinably different about this wench; she had all the animal eagerness he loved in a woman, indicating a warm, responsive partner and not just a flaccid, lifeless object on which to relieve one's lust, and yet she had a bloom of innocence about her that was unfathomably fascinating. She was still a virgin, he knew instinctively, and his belly burned all the fiercer for her.

For the next few days Mary haunted Duke Francis' thoughts though he rarely caught sight of her except when she stood, eyes downcast and attentive, behind the Queen's chair in the ballroom. Try as he might, he could not find the means to waylay her in the palace or the gardens, and his lust began to flicker into mounting anger. Who was she, this golden-haired little mouse with her soft doe's eyes, to cheat Duke Francis of his desires? Since he was fifteen he had taken every woman he wanted. Have her he must and would! He was not a man to be thwarted lightly, he, Francis, whom destiny had called to be the next King of France. Had not his mother, Louise of Savoy, seen it in the stars that her 'Caesar', as she nicknamed him, was to sit next on the throne of France? Hadn't she therefore always indulged her clever, witty, handsome son so that he could never bear frustration? Marguerite would understand. Marguerite, the loveliest, most intellectual princess he was proud to call sister. She too could not endure to be frustrated of aught she desired, and she would understand his anger.

He scowled angrily across the crowded chamber, the frown marring his brow and giving his long nose and full, sensuous lips a petulant appearance. His anger was directed at the avaricious, ageing King sitting admiringly watching his youthful Queen, and at Claude, the King's daughter and Francis' wife, who sat dutifully nearby. What a miserable, frumpish woman she was, a drab moth amongst a gay, scintillating cluster of brilliant butterflies. Who could blame a man cursed with a pudgy, lame, witless wife such as she for taking his pleasure where he could?

For a moment his gaze rested on his wife's thickening body, but the spectacle did not please him. An heir would strengthen his position when he came to rule, but Claude's appearance was even less attractive now than ever. His gaze wandered on to rest on the young Mary Tudor's body, alive and energetic as she danced. God grant the young Queen was not yet *enceinte*, for if she bore Louis a son now Francis would lose his claim to the throne. No, she was slender as a reed, her red-gilt hair flashing fire in the candlelight as she danced.

The music ceased. Mary Tudor returned to Louis, eyes a-sparkle and cheeks flushed. 'Come now, Louis, dance the galliard with me,' she pleaded. 'Come, the night is young, and I feel so gay! You have sat still for ages — come now and dance with me.'

Francis smiled sourly. Yes, he thought bitterly, tire out the old rogue so he has no energy left to climb into bed, let alone mount his Queen and beget an heir. Dance him into the grave, Mary Tudor! You have my blessing on that!

Blue eyes, eloquent and pleading, bereft the old King of his wits. He rose, stumbling, and walked out hand in hand with his tall bride into the centre of the chamber. Music from rebec and lute filled the air, but Francis' look was riveted to the shadowy figure behind the Queen's chair. Mary Boleyn, a gentle smile on her pretty face and her head tilting to the beat of the music, was gazing raptly at the dancers. Francis felt a flood of fire engorge his veins. Marguerite brushed gaily past him.

'Ho there, brother! What ails you tonight?' she quipped, then she followed his gaze curiously. 'Ah, the buxom little Boleyn filly has you ensnared, I see.' She eyed the girl appreciatively. 'Mmm. Quite a warm curvaceous armful, I should say, but hardly of your intelligence, brother,'

Francis growled. 'Of what use is intelligence in bed, sister? Do you choose your bedmates more for their wit than for their manhood?'

Marguerite's laugh trilled out, leaving behind her a wake of merriment as she swept from the chamber on her escort's arm. Francis stared fixedly across the room, sparing no glance for the King, breathless and sallow, who clutched anxiously on his wife's arm as he danced. Had he inspected his King more closely, he might have detected a tinge of grey shadowing the lined face, indicating the spectre of Death that already hovered above him.

But Francis' yearning eyes sought only the gloom of the further corner and the dim, elusive figure of the comely maid. Such a bloom she had about her, and such innocence! An amorous interlude with her would be a refreshing change from all the well-versed artistry of the French ladies. Guileless and shy, nonetheless her warmth betokened the fire beneath and with such a pupil to educate, the arts of love would take on a new and delightful tenor for him. Before long there would be no manoeuvre, no skill she had not learned. He moistened his sensuous lips in anticipation.

The dance ended. Louis, gasping and sweat-banded, flapped his hands in protestation.

'No more, my dear, I beg. I am exhausted, for it is past ten o'clock now. Surely it is time for bed?'

His pale eyes blinked beseechingly at his wife, but Mary Rose threw up her hands in horror at the suggestion.

'But you sit and rest during this next dance then, Louis my dear, while I dance with Duke Francis. Ho there! Wine for His Majesty!' she called, and came to take Francis' arm as the King tottered weakly to his chair. Behind the Queen's slender figure hovered the plumper one of her lady, Mistress Boleyn.

'Come now, my lord Duke, you will accompany me, will you not?' Mary Rose teased lightly, her eyes sparkling. 'You are not a man to tire easily, I can see, and you must agree with me it is far too early for bed yet.'

'On the contrary, Madame, there I must take issue with you.'

Mary Rose's eyebrows arched. 'You dare to argue with your Queen? You treat your life lightly to speak such treason, Duke Francis,' she quipped.

Francis led her out to the centre of the floor. 'Not I, my Queen. But I would value my manhood lightly if my mind did not turn to bed at sight of such beauty as yours.'

Mary Rose's laugh tinkled merrily. 'Smooth phrases, my lord Duke. I must warn my ladies to beware such polished flattery.'

Mary Boleyn, standing watching in the corner, caught the sound of the Queen's laugh. She felt a tinge of sadness at the sight of Francis, courteous and charming, treating the Queen as if he adored her. Yet she could not blame him, for who would spare a moment for a mouselike creature like herself when Mary Rose, lively and gay and so attractive, honoured a gentleman with her company? The moment of magic alone with Duke Francis in the darkened corridor had been shattered. Oh, that such a moment could come again!

Similar thoughts were passing through Duke Francis' mind. The vivacious young Queen stepping daintily at his side was a highly desirable woman with her teasing air and unalloyed zest for life, but danger lay in pursuing her. She might prove willing and Louis would be the easiest man in the world to dupe, and there would be undoubted pleasure in bedding Mary Rose, but the effects could prove disastrous. Discovery would render Louis mad with rage, to think of being cuckolded by his own son-in-law. Or if the pretty young Queen became pregnant, Francis could ironically find himself the means of ousting himself from the position of heir to the throne.

No, thought Francis regretfully. Much as he would enjoy caressing those lissom Tudor limbs on a silk-covered bed, it would be far safer to abandon the dream and pursue instead the plump little maid in the shadows. That way lay no danger.

The dance ended, Francis led the Queen back to her husband who sat, grey with fatigue and pathetic in his helpless indulgence. Louis gazed hopefully at Mary Rose.

'Time for bed now, beloved?'

Before the Queen could reply, Francis' eyes met the limpid, doe-like eyes of Mary Boleyn beyond and her look was one of appeal, admiration and desire.

'Very well,' said Mary Rose reluctantly. Willingly, said Francis inwardly. I'd willingly to bed with the Boleyn wench. But already she had looked away, anxious to care for her mistress who, guiding old Louis, was making to leave. Francis moved casually closer to the group and whispered in Mary's ear as she passed.

'The gallery — when you have done.'

Only a faint rush of colour to her peach-bloom cheeks indicated that she had heard; no nod, no gesture. But she would come, he was certain of it. Francis could afford a smile of amusement as he watched the King stumble away on his Queen's arm. There would be no leaping in the King's bed tonight, no making of an heir; he was far too exhausted for any such antics. Though she did not know it, the new young Queen was on Duke Francis' side in the matter of France's next ruler, so long as she continued to rob Louis of his strength in the hunt and in the ballroom. Turning his back on the unappetising sight of his wife, Claude, he left the ballroom.

Nearly an hour elapsed, Mary, tingling with anticipation, thought the Queen would never retire. Old Louis, already abed in the great bedchamber, was snoring peacefully by the time Mary Rose eventually allowed her ladies to escort her from her dressing room into the bedchamber. She smiled, chuckling with amusement as Mary turned back the silken bedcovers for her to climb in.

'I shall have no further need of help tonight, ladies. You may retire,' said the Queen. Mary fled to her own chamber to prepare for her rendezvous with Duke Francis. No time now to change her gown lest he should tire of waiting for her. Instead she brushed her hair till it gleamed silver in the candlelight, pulled her low-cut bodice yet lower to reveal the curves of her breast and bathed her face in damask-rose-water. She hastened to the gallery, her skirts rustling on the night air which lay still and silent over the sleeping Court.

She sensed his presence in the darkened corridor before she made out his broad figure in the gloom, a vital, eager warmth emanating from the shadows. Firm, strong-fingered hands reached for her body and drew her resolutely to a nearby chamber where, murmuring soft words of enticement and endearment, Francis deftly disrobed her. And in the sweet, dark, intimate hours of the night the young Duke took his fill of Mary's welcoming body, provocative and flowersoft.

Mary was enraptured. This was what she had been destined for all her life, to give and receive love, to savour the delights of the senses to the full, and with Duke Francis sensual pleasure was at its zenith.

By dawn Francis was stirring sleepily. 'It would be wisest now to return to your quarters, my sweeting,' he murmured.

Mary slid reluctantly from the bed, dressed and fled. Francis mused happily. She was a wonderful mount, pliant and eager, a virgin until now and thus she would easily school to his ways. Such warmth, such responsiveness — and not a word of cajolery or bribery. No trinkets had she begged for her favours, not even words of feigned love.

He would have her again, there was no doubt of that. Such a chance of innocent eagerness did not come his way so frequently. And moreover, she amused him with her hesitant, careful way of speaking French. Not that she had spoken in bed last night; her only sounds then had been moans of desire culminating in deep-drawn sighs of satisfaction. How refreshing to find a paramour who wasted no precious time in the inanities of conversation! Yes, a pearl indeed, this Mistress Boleyn. A rose of perfection, whom he must take care to cultivate well lest others should steal her from him.

He rolled over and, catching a whiff of the rose scent of her in the crook of his arm, he smiled contentedly and went back to sleep.

CHAPTER SEVEN

NOCTURNE

DURING the next few weeks life for Mary Boleyn was a blissful idyll. By day she savoured all the delights the lively French court had to offer, jousting and hunting, balls and masques, and by night there was the ecstasy of love-making in Duke Francis' virile arms. Life could not be sweeter, she mused, had she passed beyond the gates of Paradise.

If only there was someone to talk to, to prattle happily of her bliss! What a pity Anne was so far away in Brie, for she would have wondered at and applauded her sister's daring in taking as her first lover a noble Duke of France. Yet still, there was added piquancy in the very secrecy of their rendezvous, and Mary hugged her delicious secret close to her bosom.

So much to learn of the art of love-making, so many nuances and subtle ties of which she had never dreamed! But Francis, past master at the art, was rapidly schooling her to be as adept as himself. At the jousting Mary watched him on horseback, manly and athletic, and rejoiced when the powerful arms which by night enfolded her wielded the lance so dexterously as to bring all his opponents low. This was a man indeed, a lover of whom to be proud.

Then Mary became aware that her mistress was watching her face closely. The Queen smiled affectionately.

'Ah, I see you admire the grace of my *beau-fils*, Monsieur le Duc,' she commented. 'He cuts a fine figure indeed on horseback, does he not?'

'Indeed, Madame,' Mary replied in embarrassment,

ashamed that her face had betrayed her thoughts.

'Ah yes, Mary. Now if Francis were King of France instead of my Louis, then I think France would have no need to fret over an heir.' The young Queen's voice was low, as if speaking to herself. Mary stared in surprise and felt a little uneasy that her mistress might conceivably become her rival for Francis' attentions.

But soon her fears were stilled, for though all the women at Court seemed to blossom under Francis' gaze, their eyes warm and inviting, he seemed to have no interest in any but Mary. Each night, as the sleeping city below the castle lay steeped in midnight, she stole swiftly to his chamber and his waiting arms, and each dawn she returned, sated, to her own bed.

It was Francis who was the first to tire. Gradually he found the lure of Mary's artlessness was beginning to wane. It was Marguerite of Navarre, his extremely perceptive sister, who first noticed the slightest hint of cooling in his ardour.

'How goes it with the little English maid?' she asked him one morning as he sat writing at his desk, her fingers caressing the nape of his neck. Louise of Savoy, sitting sewing in a far window-seat, noted the gesture of affection with pleasure. They were renowned, these three, for the loving bond that held mother, son and daughter undeniably close.

Francis glanced up from his papers. 'La petite Marie? Oh, she is a willing, pliant little soul. She gives all and asks nothing in return. A cushioning feather-bed, all body and no brain. What man could ask for more?'

A knowing smile crossed Marguerite's comely face. 'That would seem to suit you, brother — for a time. But you are too witty to dally with a lackwit overlong. It will not be long, I think, before you seek out another Jeanne le Coq to whet your appetite — mental as well as physical.'

With another smile she left him and crossed the chamber

to join her mother. Francis bit his lip thoughtfully, the quill pen now idle in his hand. She was right, as ever, this shrewd sister of his. Mary's willing body and sweet winsomeness was beginning to cloy his palate a little, like one who has indulged too well in too much marchpane. Jeanne, now, the pert little wife of the advocate — she had known how to tease while yet offering him delight, to converse brightly and intelligently. Yes, Jeanne le Coq had had many advantages to offer, until another fetching beauty had distracted his eye.

Yes, the time had come for a change of partner. Marguerite was right. And since la petite Boullan had never made nor demanded protestations of love, perhaps he could disengage himself without too much trouble. Find her another handsome beau to assuage her pride, that was the answer. And with luck she would pass from one proprietor to the other with none of the tearful remonstrations he had had to endure with others in the past.

His sister stood behind his chair, noting the idle pen. She laughed softly. 'I have given you cause to think, brother? What are you debating now?'

Francis patted her hand. 'I am resolved, sister. Marie Boullan must take another lover.'

'And you? Have you selected her successor in your bed?'

He smiled mysteriously and laid a finger to his long nose. 'Not yet, but I have found no difficulty in the past.'

'Nor shall you now, I warrant. But how do you plan to dispose of your little English mare? She may break her heart over your sudden coldness.'

Francis chuckled. 'Not she. Marie gives me her body but not her heart. She is an unstintingly generous wench, and therein I think I shall find the solution to my problem.'

'How so, brother?'

'She is docile and easily suggestible, but more I shall not tell you now, inquisitive one. You must wait and see.'

'Then just assure me of one thing, Francis. It is not the

Queen, the voluptuous Mary Rose you plan to seduce next, is it? I fear for the consequences if you do.'

Francis threw back his tawny head and roared with merriment. 'Then rest assured, Marguerite. Enticing as she is, Mary Rose is not for me. Any man would be a fool to spurn the chance of bedding her, but I am not fool enough to spawn my own usurper!'

'Then I am satisfied,' his sister replied. 'Poor Louis is so infatuated with her, loading her with gifts and jewels, that it would hasten his end to know she had cuckolded him. At the pace he is living he cannot last long in any event.'

'Indeed not,' Francis murmured. 'You know what the Court is saying? That the King of England has sent a fine nag to the King of France to carry him soon and softly to hell or paradise. Soon, Mary Rose will rid France of her King and, if she conceives not, she will put me in his place. I shall not interfere with that.'

That night Mary Boleyn, her duties done, stood before the fire in her bedchamber and wriggled out of her gown. She smeared liberally all over her plump body quantities of the damask-rose perfume her mistress habitually wore, for the small amounts of money which her father sent her, grudgingly and seldom, were far from sufficient for her needs and would certainly never purchase perfume. And the heavy intoxication of the scent was essential to her now in her new life of indulging the senses to the full. Francis had often commented admiringly on the sensual aroma of her body during these last weeks.

She smiled happily at the thought of him and his hard, strong body, waiting at this moment no doubt to enfold her and keep her warm against the chilly night. She shivered a little. Despite the fire's warmth the vast chamber was draughty. So near Christmas now, and already the castle hummed with activity in preparation for the Yuletide festivities.

Toilet complete, Mary hastened along the torch-lit

passageways of the castle to the Duke's bedchamber. A smile of welcome on his full lips, he advanced to meet her, throwing wide his fur-lined bedgown to enclose her within.

Later, cloaked in midnight darkness, and sheltering in the shrouding shadows of the great fourposter bed, Mary lay content in Francis' muscular arms. Alongside her, his sinewy length sprawled across the coverlets, Francis lay wide-eyed and contemplative.

'What ails you, my Lord? You are unusually silent tonight,' Mary commented in concern. Had she, for the first time, failed to satisfy him? she fretted.

Francis groaned and stirred. 'It is nothing. Only that I grieve for a friend.'

Mary was touched. So strong, so handsome and virile and so concerned for others too. He was a fine man, this Duke of Angoulême.

'A friend in trouble?' she queried. 'If it is not presumptuous of me to ask, may I help to lift your care?'

Francis smiled gently. 'Ever kind, my little rose. But I fear you cannot help him, no more than I can. Poor Raoul. So young, so tender and so much in love with his pretty wife, and yet to be thus bereft. Naught but time can heal his wound, I fear.'

Concern for the unknown Raoul clouded Mary's gentle eyes. 'He has lost his wife?' she ventured.

'Aye, within a twelvemonth of their marriage. She died in childbirth, and the babe too.'

'Poor man. He is a close friend of your, my Lord?'

'Since childhood we have slept and ate together, rode and hunted together, for we are of an age, Raoul and I. Just think of it, *ma petite Marie* at twenty-one to feel one's life is ended. He feels no hope for the future for there is no one to love him or for him to love. No parents, no wife, no child. . . '

A rush of tenderness invaded Mary. She too knew the anguish of bereavement, the desolate feeling of love neither given nor returned to soften the solitude. She leaned on her elbow and regarded Francis' troubled face gravely.

'Oh, poor Raoul. I feel for him although I do not know him,' she said sadly. 'I would there was something I could do to help him — and thus you,' she added.

Suddenly Francis's thoughtful eyes brightened. 'Of course!' he murmured, in the tone of one who has suddenly had an idea. He turned to Mary, his voice now low and persuasive.

'You, Marie, you are the ideal person to talk to Raoul, to console and comfort him. You, with your tenderness and understanding and your loving concern for others. He is a silent fellow and broods much, but by your actions you may show him that we care.'

Mary listened, nodding, eager to please her Duke and to help one in distress.

'Then I shall introduce you to Raoul, and then leave him to your tender ministrations. I know I can rely on you to bring him solace.'

His eyes, eloquently full of gratitude, convinced Mary. It was her duty, as a humane act if nothing else, to console this poor Raoul.

'I shall not see you while you are with him,' Francis went on as he rose and dressed briskly. 'Raoul must see that you have eyes and ears only for him if he is to believe in your sympathy.'

Mary looked bewildered and strangely vulnerable, naked and solemn-eyed in the great bed. Impulsively Francis bent and kissed her. 'I shall be eternally in your debt, *petite Marie*, if you do this for me.'

'Then I shall be honoured to do as you bid,' Mary replied quietly.

It was only later as she, in company with the other ladies, laid out the gowns and unguents in preparation for the Queen's levée and toilet that she wondered what exactly she had promised to do. Francis had seemed to imply that mere words were not enough. Ah well! In time she would discover what was expected of her. Circumstances would dictate the line of action.

That evening the Queen had decreed that yet another ball should follow the day's hunt. During the course of the evening Mary saw Duke Francis approach across the crowded chamber, closely followed by a dark youth.

'Mademoiselle Marie, may I present to you my friend Raoul de Courville,' Francis said as he bowed.

The youth bowed stiffly. As she sank into a curtsey Mary regarded the bereft Raoul curiously. He was swarthy and craggily attractive with his deep-set dark eyes under thick brows and his solemn unsmiling mouth. Not quite so tall as Duke Francis but equally braod of shoulder and thigh, he was really quite a personable young man.

'I have prevailed upon Raoul to abandon his solitary mourning for the evening,' Francis said smoothly, resting his fingertips confidentially on Mary's sleeve. And then, swiftly and suavely he had made his excuses and disappeared, leaving her with the stranger. Mary turned her smile upon him. Raoul murmured some words abruptly, as if embarrassed.

'Would you prefer we leave the ballroom and talk in quiet elsewhere?' Mary offered politely.

Without a word he took her elbow and guided her from the chamber, along passages until he found a secluded alcove. There he waited until she was seated and then sat beside her. Minutes passed, and he did not speak. Mary sought for words to broach the subject of his misery.

'You must be deeply upset over your loss,' she murmured. Raoul made no reply. Mary felt uncomfortable. Francis had not warned her that the youth was thus morose and taciturn.

'Believe me, Raoul, the pain and anguish will pass. In time you will love again.'

Raoul moaned and gripped her hand tightly.

'What is it? What ails you?' she asked, affrighted at the animal cry.

'A headache — no more.' For the first time, he spoke, and Mary noted the gruff, hoarse quality of his voice, not smooth and cultured like Francis'.

'A headache? Then come, let me bathe it for you,' she said, rising and drawing him after her.

It was then, as she bent over him as he reclined on a sofa, to lay the cool, wet cloth to his brow that he seemed to unwind. Like a hawk released from the hand, his repression seemed to take flight, and he reacted hungrily to the warm, plump-bosomed figure leaning over him. Again the animal moans escaped his throat, and as Mary felt herself pressed close to his hard body, she sighed and melted submissively. Like a lost child he sought a mother to comfort him, and Mary felt her maternal feelings anxious to offer him the solace he sought.

He had none of Francis' finesse, but it was exhilerating. Mary quivered and near-fainted in his arms with pleasure. At last, when he had done, he slept as peaceful as a babe. Mary smiled contentedly. Francis would be gratified to see the smile gently curving Raoul's lips now.

It took until Christmas to console Raoul. By then he had lost his abject air of self-pity and was strutting about the castle with the same confident air as Francis and Mary was highly pleased with herself. By now she had learnt much more of the art of love than Francis had ever taught her. There seemed no end to the infinity of pleasure this pastime could offer, and when Raoul and Francis left the Court to go on a distant hunting-trip, it was touching consideration on the Duke's part to offer her yet another of his intimate friends, a laughing, fair-haired knight, to keep her company in his absence.

Thus, by the end of the eventful year 1514, Mary was revelling in the attentions of her third lover, and marvelling at the ease with which one could switch partners without apparently causing them undue heartache. Not, of course, that love-making was to her a purely animal practice, heartless and emotionless, for she felt an undoubted degree of affection for each of her partners, especially towards Francis. But it was extremely pleasant to feel protected by successive manly bodies, to savour the moments of their fleeting need and affection. With hope in her young heart she looked forward with pleasure to what the New Year would bring. Not so her mistress, Mary Rose.

'New Year's Eve,' the Queen remarked in a flat, lacklustre voice, gazing disinterestedly at her reflection in the mirror as she sat at her dressing chest. 'At midnight the new year begins and I wonder what it will bring for us, Mary. Another year of pretence and deceit like this? Of pretending to love an old dotard and to have forgotten my only love? Oh Charles, Charles, will I ever see you again?

The Queen's eyes were bright with unshed tears, and again Mary's heart swelled with pity for the girl. For all Mary Rose had appeared so vital and gay this past twelvemonth, Mary knew she still loved and longed for her beloved Charles Brandon. Misery bowed her shoulders; Mary could scarce refrain from cradling her close in comfort. Another of her ladies entered.

'Madame, the King is ready to retire,' she announced.

Mary Rose sighed and stood up wearily, 'Louis is ever ready for his bed,' she said softly as she walked slowly to the door. 'Would to God he would take to it for ever and let me free.'

New Year's Day dawned, bright and crisp. Eager to get to his bed the night before, Louis was unable to rise from it in the morning, for he was ill. As the day progressed, the feeble King realised the end was near, and sent for his confessor. By nightfall it was all over.

The young Queen's wish had been granted. King Louis XII was dead.

CHAPTER EIGHT

INTERLUDE

QUEEN Mary Rose's wish, suddenly granted, took her by such surprise that she knew not whether to weep or jubilate. Freedom was now here, or so it seemed, but when she rose from the customary week in bed of a royal widow, she realised that every eye in Court was glued to her person. Duke Francis had as yet made no move to announce his accession.

'They wait to discover whether I am *enceinte*, Mary, whether Louis has left me with child. If the weeks pass and my body swells not, Francis will act.'

But Francis acted sooner than she expected. When he strode into Court, big-bodied and confident, Mary Boleyn realised how changed he was. Regal, distant, aloof, he showed no sign of their earlier intimacy as he ignored her completely in order to speak to her mistress. The Queen dismissed Mary, and, after Francis had left, she recalled her.

'He wants to marry me, Mary. He plans to make doubly certain of the throne,' the girl said in a strained voice, her face pale as her linen cap.

Mary gasped. 'But he is already wed, Madame!'

Mary Rose sighed. 'He can put her aside, as has been done before. Louis put aside his first wife, Jeanne of France. Oh Mary! I fear this Duke Francis! I fear he is ruthless and may do me harm!'

'No, no, madame, no he, I am certain!' Mary protested. 'But you do not mean to wed him?'

'I cannot. I married Louis because my brother wished it,

but Henry promised me I should choose where I would for my next husband. And you know well who he will be, Mary.'

'My Lord of Suffolk?'

'Aye, Charles Brandon or none, I swear it. I shall write to my brother at once and ask him to fetch me home to England.'

Cold fingers of melancholy lay heavy on Mary's heart. Home, to England again, after the joyous, carefree life in France? Home to Hever and Father and a dismal, narrow life? It was a depressing prospect.

The weeks passed miserably for Mary, the Queen having bad toothache and venting her pain and worry on her luckless ladies, the weather bleak and fretful, and a constant atmosphere of tension and threat in the air at Court. In February Charles Brandon arrived in Paris, sent by King Henry to escort Mary Rose home to England. Mary Boleyn breathed again, convinced that now all would be well, at least until Hever Castle had spread its cloak of gloom over her once again.

But a few days later, without warning, the young Queen-widow sprang a totally unexpected secret on her lady-in-waiting.

'Mary, Charles and I have secretly wed,' she announced exultantly. 'Now no one can force me to marry the Duke of Flanders or Francis or anyone else!'

'But Madame — the King!' Mary gasped.

'My brother will be angry, but he will accept it,' Mary Rose said confidently, though Mary felt apprehensive on her behalf. A Queen of France to marry an English nobody without consultation — that would surely anger everyone, French and English alike. Mary was no intellectual, but it needed no clever political brain to foresee the danger in Mary Rose's impetuous action. Headstrong like all the Tudors, she cared little for the consequences, until a letter from Wolsey warned her of King Henry's displeasure.

'I shall soon sweeten Henry nonetheless,' she confided

in Mary with composure. And to Mary's horror, she despatched at once to England the Mirror of Naples, a magnificent diamond given to her by Louis.

'Madame, it is a treasured heirloom in France,' Mary protested, but to no avail. And when Wolsey's next letter spoke of King Henry's continuing wrath and his determination to have Brandon's head for his effrontery, Mary Rose calmly packing up her remaining gold plate and jewels to placate him.

Francis, learning of her actions and now the declared King of France, curtly demanded the return of the Mirror of Naples. 'It was not yours to dispose of, Madame. As Louis' widow you already receive a pension of eighty thousand francs a year, and that should suffice for your needs.'

When she refused to return either the diamond or the eighteen pearls of inestimable value, Francis grew coldly furious. Mary Boleyn slunk silently from the chamber in dread of his icy fury, but the young Queen was adamant. If she held out long enough, she felt sure King Henry would relent at last and allow her and Brandon to return safely to England.

At last, through Wolsey's careful intercession the reprieve came. Mary Rose danced excitedly about the chamber.

'We are going home, Mary! You and I and Charles, to England and to Court! Home to safety and away from intrigue and hatred, for I know the French people hate me now. Oh, isn't it wonderful!'

Mary did not share her mistress's rapture, feeling only disappointment and dismay. And it seemed a trifle ironic that at this moment a letter should arrive from Brie, from her young sister.

Anne's letter was joyful. 'I am to come to Paris to join you at Court! Is it not wonderful news? Father has arranged for me to enter the service of Queen Claude, and I am overjoyed at the prospect. Having, therefore, just written to thank him for his good offices on my behalf, I hastened to assure him that conversing with so sensible and elegant a princess will make me even more desirous of continuing to speak and write good French. I penned the letter in French myself, without Simonette's aid, to show him how I progress, and realising his concern for my honour at the wicked court, I reassured him of my resolve to lead as holy a life as he might please to desire of me.

Thus I close, dear sister, in the impatient hope that we shall be soon together in Paris. Anne de Boullan.'

Mary folded the letter sadly. How unfortunate that as Anne was to arrive, bouyant and full of hope, she was to leave under a cloud of sadness and regret.

Maytime came, lifting with its warm breezes the chill fingers of dying winter from the land and filling the air with expectancy, but out from Paris rode a cavalcade of Englishmen, escorting their Princess towards Calais and home, Parisians scorned to notice their departure, too haughty to recognise a woman who had arrived as Queen and was leaving a mere Duchess, wife to a petty English parvenu.

Only one English heart rejoiced. Just before she had mounted her palfrey, the new King of France, having made a disdainful farewell to Mary Rose, turned to her lady-in-waiting, a gentle smile now on his full lips.

'Mademoiselle Boullan, you have shown here naught but kindness and consideration for others. In return I would you may present this letter to the King of England, commending you to his care and esteem.'

Before Mary could reply, he had turned sharply and left them. In her hand lay the parchment he had given her.

Nostalgia filling her heart as the rubbish-strewn streets of Paris faded behind her, Mary had still reason to be content. Sir Thomas could not now be sullenly angry that his eldest daughter could no longer grace the court at Paris for with luck she would enter that at Greenwich instead, and with no effort on his part. For once his dull daughter had contrived an entrée on her own account.

At Calais they boarded the ship for home, the headstrong young Duchess of Suffolk and her husband, and Mary stuffed her fingers in her ears to block out the jeering cries of the French townsfolk who came to give vent to their scorn. The young Queen who had arrived in France but six months earlier to a fanfare of trumpets, made her exit to a chorus of catcalls.

'What was the paper I saw King Francis hand you before we left?' the Duchess asked Mary as her ladies prepared the cabin for her to retire. The air of curiosity was well masked beneath a casual tone.

'A letter, Madame, to your brother.'

'A letter?' Mary Rose's tone was frankly surprised and incredulous now. 'Since when has the King of France used a wench as his emissary? Is your father, Sir Thomas, no longer my brother's ambassador?'

'Madame, you misunderstand. It is but a letter of recommendation of my services.'

'Indeed?' The Duchess's eyebrows arose, a flicker of amusement curling the corners of her lips. 'Then pray let me deliver it for you, Mary, for I am like to see and be alone with my brother before you are.'

'Gladly, Madame.' Mary surrendered the letter willingly, for as yet she knew not what was to become of her. Unless King Henry or Mary Rose invited her to Court she would be doomed to return to Hever.

'You will of course accompany me to Greenwich, for I have need of your services,' Mary Rose informed her. 'What your father decides when we see him again remains to be seen.'

Mary Rose embraced her brother with tears of joy. He looked to have aged a little since their parting in Dover six months earlier, having rejoiced at the birth of a son to Catherine though the infant lived but a few hours. Yet still he was a tall, hefty giant of a man, impressively handsome with his Tudor red hair and air of leonine confidence. She hugged him heartily, glad of his forgiveness, before handing him the letter.

Henry read it in silence, then broke into a hearty roar of laughter.

'The impudence of the fellow! Hear this, Mary Rose, and he a King but for two months! "Brother of England," he says, "we commend to your care the maid Marie Boullan, daughter of your ambassador, to use with kingly love and care. Use her well, I pray, as we have done, for she is a right amiable and compassionate creature, frail and conscious of her allegiance. Her willingness to perform in one's service is highly creditable, and thus we commend this amenable maid to you, to use well and mightily as we would ourselves. To His Grace the King of England from his Brother of France. Francis." What think you of that?'

'It is very sweet of Francis,' Mary Rose remarked.

'Sweet?' Henry roared again, gales of laughter rocking his burly frame. 'Sweet, is it? You are too innocent, Mary Rose. 'Use her well,' he says — Do you not follow? 'Use her well, as we have done.' This little Boleyn wench was his mistress then, was she not?'

Mary Rose fluttered. 'I know not, Henry. I do not question my ladies as to their amours.'

'But I know. Francis is offering me one of his mistresses, no doubt to assuage her pride. Out of one royal bed into another. The girl is her father's daughter, is she not? And like Sir Thomas she is no doubt a time-server too, anxious to please in the hope of reward. God's bones, I'll have no part in Francis' worn-out affaires.'

'But Mistress Mary is not like that!' Mary Rose protested vehemently. 'She is a sweet, undemanding soul, amaible and compassionate as Francis says. She seeks no favours, of that I am sure, no matter who her father is or what his character. I wish to keep her about me at Court.'

'As you will. But I shall have no need of her services, I assure you. I am well satisfied with my Bouncing Bess.'

'Bess?' Mary Rose's voice rose questioningly. In her absence she had lost track of court gossip, but this sounded interesting. Henry, married to his squat, over-pious wife for six years now, had not been known to take a mistress before. He had evidently changed more than she realised during her absence in France. 'Who is Bess, Henry?'

'Her name is Elizabeth Blount, one of the Queen's ladies. And she is all I desire in a woman, plump and inviting. Of course Catherine knows naught of her for we meet only when I hunt, in some remote pavilion, so I beg you maintain a discreet silence on the subject.'

Remembering Henry's recent forgiveness concerning her marriage, Mary Rose nodded in agreement.

Henry called for a servant to pour out wine in golden goblets. He leaned confidentially across to Mary, lowering his hearty voice to a murmur that was filled with amusement.

'So you see, you may keep your precious Mary Boleyn to yourself, sister. I am well provided for and have no need of Francis' cast-offs.'

And screwing the crackling parchment into a ball, he flung it into the heart of the big fire.

CHAPTER NINE

LEGATO

MARY ROSE soon began to tire of life at Henry's Court at Placentia, and before long she made preparations to leave.

But she took care of Mary Boleyn before she left, entrusting the maid to the care of Queen Catherine, to continue in her service as a lady-in-waiting. Sir Thomas made no objection. He was as content to have his feeble-minded daughter in service to the Queen of England as in that of the ex-Queen of France. While still at Court and in the public eye there was still a chance for her to secure a good husband for herself, despite the rumours which had followed her from France implying her easy ways with men.

So Mary sat, glancing up every now and then from her embroidery to regard the Queen's impassive face. Oh, how bored she was! Life was incredibly dull at Court since Mary Rose had gone. True, the gallants watched her appreciatively, aware of the promise that lurked under her golden-blonde exterior, curved and inviting, and Mary dimpled attractively in response to their glances. But Queen Catherine's rigid routine for her household offered little opportunity to indulge the passions that seethed unrequired in Mary's breast. She muttered resentfully to her companion Margaret who stitched laboriously at the same length of linen.

'Only regard our Queen, Margaret, and see how aged she looks! And she behaves like an ancient dame who fears death at any moment, the way she arises before dawn to hear Mass, dragging us with her, and spending hours every day on her knees in prayer. How can we find the time to dance and coquette when she has us spending so much time embroidering altar-cloths for her abbeys and churches? We too will be old and grey before long.'

Margaret nodded. 'But she has cause to look careworn and to pray. So many lost babes, and still she hopes to have a son for His Grace.'

'She? She looks far too old!'

'She is but thirty-one, despite her grey hairs.'

Mary snorted. 'And the King is but twenty-four. He should have a young and fertile wife, not his brother's widow so much older than himself.'

Queen Catherine looked up from her sewing. 'Come, ladies,' she said in a soft, far-away voice. 'It is time for us to go to the chapel again.'

With a sigh Mary put down her embroidery needle and followed. The prayers, she felt, were all in vain. But before long the Queen glowed with new hope. She was pregnant again, and this time, God willing . . . .

The child was born on a wintry day in 1516, a daughter, but God be praised, this child was healthy and would live. The Queen, a little greyer and more sallow after the ordeal of the birthing, resumed her pious regime. Mary regarded her speculatively.

'I wonder the King, so handsome and virile, finds pleasure in such a wife,' she confided thoughtfully to Margaret. The lady giggled and blushed.

'Then you have not heard of his — dalliance?'

Mary was startled. 'King Henry?' Dallies with another woman? I had no conception of it. Pray, tell me who she is, I beg you!'

A swift nudge in the ribs told Mary to be quiet. Another lady of the Queen's train had entered the chamber and was busy scouring the contents of a closet. Having found what she sought, she left. Margaret giggled uncontrollably.

'Speak of the devil, they say. That was she.'

'Lady Elizabeth?'

'Aye, Bess Blount. It was a well-kept secret for a time, I hear, but now all the Court knows of it, and I doubt not but that it has come to the Queen's ears too.'

'Oh, surely not, for why does not Her Grace dismiss her?'

Margaret shrugged. 'Who knows? Perchance she is willing to turn a blind eye so long as it keeps her beloved husband happy. So long as he comes to her bed to make an heir, she is content to keep trying.'

Another thought crossed Mary's mind. 'But Elizabeth is betrothed to Sir Gilbert Taillebois, and they are soon to wed.'

'That is no reason for matters to change,' Margaret commented drily. Mary was amazed. Meg knew far more of the ways of kings and courtiers than she, but even so it seemed remarkably scandalous.

Elizabeth Blount was wed and left the court, for a manor named Jericho in Essex which, rumour had it, was a gift from the King. When the young King departed frequently on hunting trips in Essex, laughing remarks fluttered about the Court about the walls of Jericho falling down, surrendering to the omnipotent King.

Time slipped by, though to impatient Mary Boleyn, who felt her wings severely clipped by the constraint of the Queen's regime, time dragged slowly by. Wistfully she yearned for the freedom and light-heartedness of the French Court and the coquetry and love-making which, it seemed, were now forever to be denied to her.

Occasionally she was freed from her duties long enough to visit Hever and Lady Beth, who was overjoyed to see her again and who asked endless questions about the Court and the Queen. Mary, knowing her stepmother fondly believed her to be unfathomably happy at Greenwich, had not the heart to disappoint her, and answered her questions patiently.

'No, stepmother, Her Grace does not subscribe to the latest fashions. She wears still the wide farthingale and lace mantillas she brought with her from Spain. Yes indeed, she is a most pious lady, rising at five in the morning to hear Mass.'

In her turn she plied her stepmother with questions about her family. Her brother George she saw on occasion at Greenwich, for he was a lyrist now to the King, but of Anne she had heard no news of late.

'I am surprised she has not written to you,' Lady Beth remarked. 'She has been most diligent in the service of Queen Claude, rising early and working hard at the loom and embroidery frame, but she bemoans the lack of gentlemanly company. Queen Claude, it seems, considers gentlemen a distraction. However, Anne seems quite light-hearted. She wrote me last of a new fashion she had devised which the other Court ladies are copying — a velvet cape, a bourrelet I believe she called it, hanging in points with a little bell attached to each. Imagine that, Mary, jingling with bells as one walks, like a cow! However, she says she hopes life will shortly become more eventful, as King Francis has suggested she might like to enter the service of his sister Marguerite, Duchess of Alençon, and Anne seems very happy at the prospect.'

Mary reflected. She too would be happy to be noticed again by the dashing Francis, and for a moment she felt a flicker of envy for her sister's good fortune.

On her return to Placentia Mary found the palace throbbing with the latest item of gossip. Lady Elizabeth Taillebois had given birth to a son, and all the world knew it was the King's child and not her husband's. Did not the babe's flaming Tudor-gold hair confirm it? Even from the convent in Essex whither Lady Elizabeth had hastened to give birth, the news of the child and his appearance had already reached the Court.

The King was in hearty good humour that night, and declared a banquet should be held. The ladies in the mess-hall whispered excitedly.

'His Grace is in high good humour now he has proved himself.'

'Proved himself?'

'Aye, that he can beget a healthy boy child after all. The Queen's failure to provide him with an heir was giving him cause to doubt it.'

'Then I'll warrant Lady Elizabeth will be yet more in his good graces now.'

'Aye, she can ask what she will of the King now. Manors, jewels, titles, what she will. I've never seen His Grace so happy as he is tonight.'

'He'd be happier yet if the child had been born to him in wedlock.'

'True, but now he knows he can beget a healthy son, he'll try the Queen the harder for it.'

The King's manner at the banquet seemed to prove their words. He laughed gaily and called to the musicians to play his own latest song, lately composed. The Queen sat silent, and Mary noted her strained expression and that she barely touched a morsel. If she was not yet again pregnant, the greyness could only mean she too had heard of Elizabeth Taillebois' child.

But the King was exhilarated. Mary gazed with pleasure upon him, his happiness causing his blue eyes to sparkle and his handsome face aglow with a radiance she had never seen before. He seemed utterly unaware of his wife's blank weariness, calling repeatedly for more songs and more wine.

Eventually, having eaten his fill, he sprang on to the table, causing Queen Catherine to start back in alarm. Tankard upraised and his eyes irradiated with joyous delight, he called above the musicians' melody.

'A toast, my friends, to my Queen and our future son,' he roared. 'To the Queen!'

The company drank in assent. 'And now a hunting dance, and to the winner the spoils!'

He seized a maid about the waist and, waving a signal to the musicians above in the gallery, he began a prancing dance, showing off his calves and lifting the maid clean off the floor. Mary watched him enraptured. So fine a man, such strength in the muscles and such wild, gay abandon she could appreciate. Here was a man with whom she could enjoy sharing the zest for life he obviously displayed. So like Duke Francis, and yet so much more a man.

Other dancers crowded about him, blocking him from her view, and then he reappeared, the fine grey silk doublet slashed with blue now hanging from his back. Mary watched in amusement.

'Seize your chance, my friends,' his laughing voice could be heard above the laughter. His jewel-studded cap vanished. Seconds later he reappeared, beaded with sweat and still laughing, with his shirt awry and undone, and then he fled through the open doorway, shrieking courtiers in pursuit.

'His Grace is in good humour this evening,' the Queen commented quietly. Mary hung her head.

'Indeed, ma'am.'

'I feel somewhat chilly. Pray fetch me a wrap, Mary.'

Mary left the chamber and hastened along a now empty corridor. Near a curtained doorway she noticed a glint on the floor and bending to look closer, she found a silver button. Picking it up, she examined it curiously. It was a button from the King's doublet.

A low voice at her elbow, laughter under its gentle tones, startled her. 'You too sought a souvenir of me, mistress?'

She turned sharply. King Henry, his red-gold hair tumbled and awry and his chest now bare of any clothing, stood watching her, his muscular arms akimbo and his great legs astride.

'Indeed no, Your Grace! That is, I was about to . . . I

was on an errand for Her Grace.'

'So you did not join the battle for a memento?' His eyes gleamed, his handsome head cocked to one side in question.

'No, Your Grace.'

'I am disappointed, Mistress Boleyn. I have a mind to have all the fairest ladies of the Court seeking my favours.'

Mary dimpled and blushed with pleasure. It was gratifying that the King, whom she admired so, was paying compliment to her.

'Then if I may, I shall keep the button, sire.'

'Do so, mistress. And one day, perchance, you shall have another souvenir of me. But I must return. Get about your business on the Queen's behalf.'

He strode swiftly away, leaving Mary to puzzle as to his meaning as she continued on her way. It could not have been gallantry on his part, for he had then dismissed her abruptly about her business. A pity, she sighed, It would be so entertaining to coquette with the personable young King.

Dismissing the thought as impractical, Mary went on to the Queen's bedchamber. But in the course of the next few weeks the same thought came unbidden to her mind again. Was it her fancy that she thought the King's eye rested thoughtfully on her just a second longer than usual as she saw to the Queen's wants? Was it imagination that he appeared unexpectedly while she ministered to Catherine, far more frequently than hitherto? It was Catherine herself who commented on it at last.

'His Grace comes more often to see us now, Mary, do you notice?'

'I had thought it, Ma'am.'

The Queen pressed her hands together, as if in unconscious prayer. 'With God's grace he will look to us more kindly now. I understand his other — distractions — were but of passing interest, and now, God willing, all will be well betwixt us.'

Stupified, Mary made no rejoinder. Had the Queen known all along of Bess Blount then, and held her peace? If so, she was a compassionate woman indeed, and Mary respected her the more. Gossip in the mess-hall confirmed the news. Bess Blount, paid off with a pension and a title for her infant Henry Fitzroy, was now no longer the King's favourite. Tiring of his love, he was seeking another diversion.

'Think you he will remain faithful to the Queen now?'

'I doubt it. What King confines himself to one infertile pasture when the whole country is his to command?'

'Who next then, I wonder?'

'Any pretty face and rounded bosom that falls under his glance, and as he has picked from the Queen's entourage before, it could be one of us again.'

Giggles and speculation rang happily in the high-raftered chamber, each hoping and plotting how she could best profit from the situation. Many a lowly maid had come by a title from a grateful sovereign, simply by being at court and readily accessible at the right moment. Only one fair head, bent in thought as she wielded her knife over the roast beef, harboured no thought of gain. If only the King would take a fancy to me, Mary Boleyn thought blissfully. Such a man I would give all I had. Such a man would give me infinite pleasure in return. Youth, vigour, strength, and beauty — he had all that was most desirable in a man.

It was a delicious daydream, suddenly shattered when Margaret, leaned across the table. 'It will be me, Mall, or no one. I shall have the King as my bedmate ere the week is out, I vow.'

Mary's wide eyes gazed back at her. 'How can you be so sure, Meg?'

Margaret's dark eyes twinkled as she leaned nearer. 'Tell not a soul or I'll cut your heart out, Mary Boleyn. Last night — in the gardens — he caught me and kissed me down by the yews. He pinched me and said I was a comely filly who needed a stout stallion.'

Margaret's eyes were dark with triumph. Mary trembled, her blood leaping in her veins at the thought of Margaret and the King lying together, and she longed desperately to take Margaret's place.

'But he meant no more than to jest, perchance? He may never approach you again.' It was wishful thinking, perhaps, but Mary fought to banish the mental picture of Henry's hands on Meg's smooth body.

'A jest, is it?' Margaret laughed softly. 'Then why am I to attend His Grace at midnight in a secret place? Take care, Mary Boleyn, for you hold the secret of a future Duchess belike.'

Mary pushed her plate sharply away, a thick feeling of nausea filling her throat. It was not the fact of the pair making love that disgusted her, but Margaret's intention to reap rewards from her actions.

Mary's short-lived daydream, fragile and ethereal, of herself and the laughing, gilt-haired Henry lying contentedly entwined, was shattered into fragments.

CHAPTER TEN

OVERTURE

A FEELING akin to jealousy pricked Mary's heart, and she pushed the unpleasant sensation sharply away. Why should she feel jealous? Unless, as she began to suspect, she had fallen victim to the powerful charms of this blond young giant, this genial, hearty man who, even if he were not King, would have stolen the hearts of every maid who encountered him.

Wistfully she watched his great broad back as he laughed at some jest with his courtiers. To Margaret would go the pleasure of caressing those muscular shoulders, to Margaret the joy of receiving his surreptitious kisses. Anxiously she watched Margaret's pretty face for the tell-tale radiance to dawn, betraying the happiness she had found in the King's arms.

But a day passed, then two, then three, and no such glow came to irradiate Meg's pale face. On the contrary, her lips drooped in sadness and her eyes were bleared as if with tears.

'What ails you, Margaret?' Mary asked in concern, anxious lest the King's attentions had not proved all Margaret had expected, but the maid only shook her head, her lips compressed, and refused to answer. It was another of the Queen's ladies-in-waiting who explained.

'His Grace sent a message she was not to attend him after all. Margaret is distressed because she does not know in what way she offended him.'

That the transgression was not Margaret's Mary was to learn from her brother. George Boleyn, looking taller and more darkly handsome than ever to his admiring sister, overtook her in the gardens where she had been walking in the sunshine with the Queen.

'What's this? Her Grace has left one of her ladies, and her most beautiful one at that, to walk down shady yew alleys alone? Does she no longer fear for your virtue?' he teased. Mary smiled. He spoke just as he used to in the old days, back at Hever before Court and France had separated them. George at least, though he had been obliged by Father to marry that acid Jane Rochford, appeared to have changed but little since the carefree days of childhood.

'Her Grace complained that the sun's heat was causing her head to ache and returned to her chamber, thus for once I am left unemployed for a time.'

'You are not required to bathe the royal brow?'

'No, she bade Lady Margaret attend her.'

George smiled wryly. 'The Lady Margaret? No doubt she too has need of a cold compress to cool her fever. I hear the King set fire to her tender heart, then declined to quench the flames.'

'How did you know? I believed it was we women who bandied gossip, but you are quick with the news,' Mary replied. 'Who told you of it?'

'His Grace himself. It was last night when I attended him at his retiring. Such a ceremony, what with the yeomen searching the bed and kissing the pillows! To be short, I was curious as to why he had bidden me attend him then, and when he had donned his nightgown and cap and dismissed the gentlemen of the bedchamber, he bade me linger. I wondered why I had been singled out for such privilege.'

'And did you discover?' Mary breathed in excitement. 'Are you to be advanced, knighted perhaps?'

George chuckled. 'If I am, he did not speak of it. He told me instead of his passing interest in Lady Margaret.'

Mary's round eyes regarded him in surprise. 'Why you,

George? I did not know you were His Grace's confidant.'

'Nor I, little sister, but let me tell you what befell. He told me his interest in the lady had waned rapidly since his eye had fallen on another and far more pleasing maid. He could not be satisfied with the one while the other tantalised him so.'

'Another? Oh tell me, George, who is she?'

Her brother's eyes, dark and warm, crinkled at the corners as he made her wait, breathless, for his reply.

'You cannot guess?'

Mary's fair curls shook vigorously.

'Then I'll tell you. It is you, my sweeting. The King has a mind to bed with you.'

Mary's hand flew to her mouth to stifle the gasp that came unbidden. She sank on to a nearby bench, feeling her knees weaken beneath her and her head giddy with shock.

'Come now,' George laughed softly as he sat beside her, 'is this the time for virginal prudery? I have heard it whispered that you have surrendered your favours before now, and often, while in France.'

'The King — desires me?' Mary whispered, unable to believe the words as she spoke them, but savouring the feeling of pleasure that began to rise in her.

'Most heartily, and will not rest till he has you.'

Mary hesitated. Why then had not King Henry made approaches to her himself, as he had done to Bess Blount? It was not like the King, usually so direct and uncomplicated, to send an envoy on his behalf. She raised perplexed blue eyes to her brother.

'Did His Grace bid you speak of this to me?'

George chuckled again, his dark head thrown back in amusement. 'Lord, no! He believes you a pure and innocent maid, and would have spoken to Father had he been here instead of in France on the King's business.'

'To Father?' Mary was even more puzzled. It was not usual for a man to ask another if he might seduce his daughter, and since the King was already wed it could not be to ask for Mary's hand.

'Aye, of course. He knows he holds Father in the palm of his hand, that Father will do aught to please the King in order to advance himself. A little favour, Sir Thomas, your buxom daughter in our royal bed, and who knows what favours we may not heap on you in reward. Our King is a shrewd man, Mary, if unsubtle, and he knows how to manage Father if no one else can.'

'I see.' Mary pondered over George's words. 'Then why, if he wanted Father's approval, did he speak to you?'

'As his son I stand in Father's stead in his absence, head of the Boleyn household and thus in charge of you. Moreover, I could pave the way with Father when he returns.'

'And do you approve of my becoming the King's mistress?' Mary asked solemnly. George smiled.

'You will do as your heart dictates, Mary, and not as I bid you. But I admit I would not decline the favours His Grace would undoubtedly show to me too in the event of your — agreeability.'

George fell silent, his brow furrowed in contemplation. Mary was appreciative of his reserve, his determination not to force her hand but to let her act as she felt best. For a time she too sat silent, staring up at the lattice-work of branches above them and watching the sunlight darting between them with the silent rapidity of fish in a garden pool. Hands folded demurely in her lap, she wondered how she could sit so still and apparently controlled when within her surprise and delight and anticipation clamoured. She turned to George, debating how best to tell him, not that she repelled the King's dishonourable advances, but that she welcomed them.

'George, I — that is to say — I am grateful to you for your concern. But — must we wait to discuss the matter with Father?'

George shrugged. 'He would expect it of us, but if you feel strongly that you must deny His Grace, then do so, now. If we lay the matter before Father, he will demand it of you as your duty to him, to sacrifice yourself to the King.'

Mary smiled happily. 'Then I am glad that I may combine my duty as a daughter with my own pleasure, the more so if it will enhance Father's position and yours.'

George turned and stared at her, disbelieving. 'You mean — you will accede to the King's request?'

'With pleasure, brother.'

'It does not offend you?'

'On the contrary, it delights me. I have long admired His Grace. Are you ashamed of me, George?'

George embraced her heartily. 'Not I, Mall. You were always a maid who spoke what was in her heart. There is no dissembling in you.'

Mary blushed. 'I fear I am clumsy for I never could hide what I felt. Unlike Anne, who has such a clever way with words.'

Her brother squeezed her close. 'That is what is so endearing about you, Mall. So simple, sweet and honest. None who know you can help but love you. Tell me now, am I to report to His Grace that I have spoken to you of the matter and that you are willing?'

Mary reddened furiously. 'Oh George, that seems so shameless and indelicate! Would it not be better if you said that you, as head of the household, had considered the matter and agreed? Then if His Grace approaches me, he will find that I am willing too.'

George hesitated, stroking his beard as he considered. 'Very well,' he said at length. 'I think it were best you and he should meet at Hever, out of the reach of Court gossip, I shall suggest to His Grace that he finds some pretext to send you home.'

Mary was alarmed. 'Home — to Hever! Oh, George! I

should not wish to forgo Court life and live only at Hever henceforth!'

'For a time only,' her brother hastened to reassure her. 'Once you and the King are well acquainted, he will no doubt arrange your return. Go now, before the Queen becomes curious about your absence. I shall report to His Grace.'

'And then tell me how he responds?'

George smiled, that gentle, teasing smile she knew so well. 'I doubt I shall need to, sweetheart. Undoubtedly the next move in the game is the King's.'

The move came swiftly. The very next evening as Mary lay out the Queen's bedgown on the high bed, Queen Catherine turned from the mirror and, with a wave of her hand, dismissed the lady-in-waiting who had been brushing out her hair.

'Come here, Mary, let me look at you,' the Queen order-ed. Mary approached her timidly and for the first time she felt a prick of conscience at what she had agreed to do. The Queen put a finger under Mary's chin and lifted her face to the light. 'His Grace commented today that I had perhaps been working you too hard, child, for he said you looked wan. Are you overtired, Mary?'

'Indeed no, Ma'am. You are most gracious.'

'He said he liked to see winsome maids about me, but that your beauty was faded. In his opinion you are in need of wholesome country air.'

Mary hung her head. 'His Grace is most kind.'

'He is an observant man, on occasion. Mmm, perhaps you do look a little tired. How long is it since you saw your mother, Mary?'

'Some months, Ma'am.'

'Then do you prepare to return home to Kent at once. A week or two at Hever should soon restore the colour to your cheeks. Now begone, child, for I must pray.'

Thanking her, Mary withdrew. So soon it was to begin!

King Henry had wasted no time in paving the way according to George's suggestion. Now Mary began to feel uneasy, a feeling of guilt at betraying her kindly mistress mingled with trepidation at what she had begun. Now she had spoken, now the King had arranged their meeting, it was too late to think again.

Oh, what had she done, impulsive creature that she was? Would she live to regret this decision, to find the position of King's mistress too unwieldy for her simple wits? If only there were someone to confide in and discuss the matter, some understanding friend or relative! If only Anne were here; she, with her analytical mind and shrewd wits would know best how to act.

But there was no one, so Mary went to bed with her secret unshared, spending the best part of the night sleepless and biting her lip in inward turmoil. At dawn she rose and prepared for the journey home to Hever.

George was in the courtyard to bid her godspeed, the grey light of dawn giving his dark young face a falsely aged look, but his smile was one of pure contentment.

'Prepare well, Mall. Deck yourself out in your prettiest gowns at Hever, for in two days he will come,' he murmured as he helped her mount up. 'His Grace is to go hunting in Kent, so bid Mother prepare.'

Lady Beth was both startled and overjoyed to see her stepdaughter so unexpectedly. She came bustling up from the kitchens, her rosy face speckled with flour.

'I was supervising the preserving of our best quinces and peaches,' she explained with an embarrassed smile, guilty at being caught cooking when her fine daughter came home from Court. 'But I shall order your chamber aired at once. And a hearty meal, for you must be famished, child. Come, let me give you wine while all is being done.'

Mary bided her time, giving the poor woman time to overcome her agitation before announcing the news she knew would drive Lady Beth frantic with anxiety. It was after supper when the servants had cleared the dishes away to the ambry, that Mary smiled across the hearth to her stepmother.

'Mother, I have yet more news for you.'

'Yes, child? Is it George — is he to come home too?'

'No, mother. Yet more splendid company still. His Grace the King is to come into Kent to hunt, and he expressed a desire to stay here with us.'

Lady Beth started from her chair. 'The King?' Here, at Hever, and your Father away in France? Oh, Lord have mercy! How am I, a mere country-woman, to entertain the King?'

Mary spoke soothing words. 'Have no fear, Mother, I am well used to His Grace's ways, and I know well what dishes he prefers. I shall go to the kitchens tomorrow and all will be as he would wish it. Father shall not be ashamed of us.'

This last phrase was to reassure Lady Beth for Mary knew how she feared to displease her exacting husband. But Lady Beth was still ruffled.

'But how shall I talk to him, Mary? He is used to fine Court phrases and flattery and I know naught of such things.'

Mary knelt at her feet and put her hand on the older woman's. 'Be your own sweet self, Mother, and he will love you as we do. Even a King tires of smooth-tongued flatterers at times and is glad of simple honesty such as yours. All will be well, I know it.'

Yet though Lady Beth seemed appeased, Mary wished in her heart that she too believed that all would be well. What would be the outcome of the King's visit? Would he perchance be displeased by Mary? She, like Lady Beth, was no match for the brilliant, witty women at Court and perhaps the King would find no attraction in such a dim-witted wench, no matter how comely.

Yet again Mary Boleyn slept little that night.

CHAPTER ELEVEN

CRESCENDO

I<small>T</small> was hot and heavy, the air over the castle blue-grey in threatening sultriness. Mary, exhausted from hurrying about making preparations for the King's entertainment, slumped in a chair, her head throbbing from effort.

Lady Beth bustled in, humming as she re-arranged the flowers in the pewter bowl for the fourth time. She stood back at last, frowning.

'Think you the King likes roses, Mary? Or would he prefer more homely flowers? I cannot think what the nobility at Court would wish, but you should know.'

Mary smiled feebly. 'It matters little, Stepmother. He will scarce notice the flowers, only you and your kindliness, and whether his bed is soft and the venison tender.'

'Lady Beth, smoothed the back of her hand across her forehead. 'My head quite aches, if not from excitement then it must be a thunderstorm approaching.'

The first drops spattered the paved terrace outside the window. The sky lowered ominously, and a faint blush of green tinged the air.

A distant horn sounded, Lady Beth stood, arm upraised, startled. 'Harken! A hunting horn!'

Mary leapt to her feet. 'Oh Mother! I am not ready! Just look at my gown, all spattered with grease!'

Lady Beth gained control of herself. 'Go you at once to your chamber and change. I shall receive His Grace if you are not down. But make haste!'

Mary fled, but even as she reached her room the clatter of hoof-beats below and hoarse cries met her ears. By now the rain was dashing heartily against the window.

Pulling a fresh gown over her head and lacing it swiftly, Mary crossed to the window. Between the meshed pattern of raindrops, she could see him, tall and merry as he handed over his horse to an ostler. In hunting green, his cloak clinging damply to his broad shoulders, he looked as regal and comely as she had ever seen him.

'Be sure to take the venison directly to the kitchens,' he called loudly, shaking his gilt curls free of the glistening rain droplets before entering the house. Mary, trembling with exhilaration at the sight of him, strong and beautiful as the god Dionysius fresh from the chase, smoothed her pale hair before descending to the great hall.

Lady Beth's nervousness at meeting the King was forgotten in her concern for him. 'But Your Grace must put off those wet clothes and change instantly, or you'll catch your death,' she was clucking. King Henry smiled indulgently.

' 'Tis naught, Madam. A summer shower, only,' he was saying, spreading his hands to the log fire Lady Beth had ordered despite the heat of the day.

'I can see steam rising from your breeches, sire,' Lady Beth insisted, her hands thrown up in horror. 'Do you have a change of apparel, Your Grace, or shall I see what I can procure for you?'

Mary, standing listening at the head of the staircase, could not resist smiling. Even the King could not take offence at her kindly step-mother's solicitude.

'Madam, you are most kind,' his deep voice boomed. 'I shall order my gentleman to unpack a change of clothing for me presently. But first, if you please, I should relish a goblet of wine for I am parched with thirst.'

'To be sure, Sire. Forgive me if I forget my manners.' Lady Beth was pouring the wine herself as Mary came down, treading carefully and her head held high.

Henry rose at once. 'Mistress Mary, I am enchanted to

see you,' he said politely as he held out his hand. Mary took it, sinking into a low curtsey as she did so. Excitement, nervousness and desire tingling inside her like a wayward skein of wool, she looked into his eyes and read therein the desire that matched her own. Lady Beth, fortunately, was too preoccupied with the wine to notice. Henry took the goblet gratefully and tossed off the contents. Lady Beth refilled it smilingly.

Seated by the fire, the King talked amicably with Lady Beth of how well the corn was ripening in the Kentish fields and how fine the hunting hereabouts, but all the while Mary sat silent, feeling the power of his eyes as they roved over her from the blue silk of her kirtle up to her creamy bosom and averted face and down again. Within she shivered. His gaze was magnetic and compelling. For two pins she could have thrown herself into his arms there and then but for the fear of offending Lady Beth's sense of propriety.

'And by the by, I have good news for you, Madam,' he said at length. 'Your husband is even now on his way homeward. I have given orders that just as soon as he reaches the Court he is to follow me here, so he should arrive home at Hever very soon.'

Mary saw the quick flicker in her stepmother's eyes. The poor woman, already distraught with the worry of entertaining His Grace, was now worrying over her lord's possible criticism. He would be frantic with anger if all was not perfection in his home while it harboured the King as a guest.

Almost as though he sensed her unease, Henry spoke again, his eyes leaving Mary for an instant to travel about the great chamber. 'Indeed, he should be here presently, and I shall have then the opportunity to tell him how his home pleases me, and his gracious lady-wife and beauteous daughter likewise.'

Lady Beth's plump cheeks dimpled in pleasure. 'But my

lord will not forgive me if Your Grace has caught a cold, Sire, so if you please I will show you now to your chamber.'

Henry rose obediently, his long legs causing him to tower above the two women who stood, rapt, lost in admiration of him. 'Madam, I follow, he said simply. And though he followed his hostess dutifully up the great oak staircase, Mary felt his slumbrous gaze still dwelling upon her, and was filled with delight. As he disappeared from view she regained her wits, hastening away to see that the servants had laid the table for their honoured guest with all the finest plate and napkins.

Throughout the meal, though his lips phrased only polite words of conversation to Lady Beth, Henry's eyes still spoke to Mary, causing her such agitation that she could barely eat. Lady Beth's quick eye took note of her lack of appetite.

'Why do you not eat, Mary? Is the venison not to your liking, my dear? Or are you not feeling well?' she asked in concern.

'No, no, Mother, it is delicious but I am not hungry. The thunderstorm, no doubt,' Mary murmured apologetically. Lady Beth's gaze fluttered to the King. It would be ungracious to send her daughter to lie down, neglectful of one's duty as a hostess. Once again, Henry intervened.

'Pray let Mistress Mary retire and rest a while,' he suggested amiably. 'Now the rain has ceased and the sun begins to shine anew, I shall return to the forest to hunt until dusk.'

Mary felt a flicker of disappointment. He was not over-anxious for her company, then, if the hunt held more attraction for him. She raised her eyes to see he was smiling across the table to her.

'And if I might suggest it, Mistress Mary, a walk later, through Hever's pretty gardens and beyond into the wood might finally dispel the last traces of your headache,' he said. Her spirits rose. Perhaps he intended to 'intercept her there, far from Lady Beth's eyes.

Thus, late in the afternoon, long after King Henry had cantered out of the courtyard again, calling to the hounds and quipping with his companions, Mary tied on her cap and sauntered out as nonchalantly as she could into the gardens. Once out of sight of Lady Beth, who stood waving from an upper window, she hastened her steps towards the wood.

For the first hour, as she strolled among the trees, eager and full of anticipation, she felt buoyant with hope. Then, as the sun began to dip behind the trees and the shadows lengthened across the grass, she began to shiver a little as the evening breezes caught her bared arms. The half-light began to plan tricks with the darting shadows under the branches, and Mary recollected the childhood tales she had heard tell of pixies and elves who played pranks on mortals who strayed in their woodland home by night. Perhaps, after all, he would not come and she had best return. Perhaps she had wishfully read a meaning into his suggestion that he had not intended. Perhaps the King was already back at Hever, anxious for his supper and harassed by Lady Beth fretting over Mary's delay.

The shadows grew deeper. Fearfully Mary decided she dare no longer stay and, turning sadly towards home, she began to retrace her steps. The bracken bent crisply under her footsteps and she heard no other sound save evening birdsong, so it took her breath away to catch sight of a figure, gleaming silver in the dusk, leaning against a tree trunk a few paces ahead of her.

The figure uncurled itself and stood upright and as Mary stood trembling, her hands to her mouth, it spoke.

'Mistress Mary, I feared I had missed you.'

It was he! With a fierce leap of joy she recognised the deep timbre of Henry's voice, and the silver doublet he had donned to go hunting. He came towards her, his hands outstretched.

'Your mother frets that you are out so late,' he said quietly, taking her hands in his.

'I am sorry. I did not know you had returned, Sire.'

'We approached Hever from the far side. Have you been waiting long here?' Mary nodded dumbly. 'For me?' She hesitated before inclining her head again. Henry smiled and drew her closer. Her fingertips, pressed against the crisp white cambric shirt which protruded through the slashed sleeves, could feel the sinewy strength of his arms beneath, and the blood pounded in her veins.

Now would come the honeyed words of wooing, the urgent phrases such as she used to hear on Francis' lips, the voice hoarse with passion. Mary closed her eyes in blissful expectancy, longing for his strong hands to join the persuasive argument. At once the hands responded to her wish.

'Mary, little beauty, I am on fire for you,' his words came in the darkening air. 'I have such need for you.'

Thrilled, Mary nonetheless stayed his questing hand. 'Here, Sire? Out of doors, when we are stayed for?'

Henry laughed softly. 'Why not al fresco, my sweeting? Is it not natural for all God's beasts? Come now, deny me not, for I have been patient over-long already.'

She stroked a finger along his beard, laying it at last on his lips. 'If supper awaits, there will be eyebrows raised at our lateness, Sire. Tongues may wag.'

Henry snorted and drew back. 'Eyebrows? Tongues? Who would dare to question the King's movements? I will have no subject so disloyal, and you, Mistress Boleyn, you would not be so unruly as to defy me, would you?'

'Defy you I would never do, nor deny you, Sire.'

Henry sighed as he drew her close again. 'Then come, sweetheart,' he murmured, tossing his cloak on the grass. 'Here is a sweet couch beneath the trees, and by starlight we shall find contentment, you and I.'

He knelt, pulling Mary with him, and as she yielded to his firm strength a sudden cry and crackling in the undergrowth disturbed the quiet of the wood. In the distance the light of torches could be discerned, and a running figure coming towards them. Henry rose at once, his handsome face thunderous in anger.

'Damnation!' he muttered furiously.

'Your Grace! Mistress Boleyn!' a voice called.

'Who calls me? What is it?' Henry demanded loudly. Mary straightened her gown swiftly. The figure approached. It was a servant from the castle.

'Sire! Mistress Boleyn! My lady sent me to find Mistress Mary, but I see you have found her already, Your Grace.'

'Indeed. But why such urgency, man? The lady was safe in my keeping.'

'Supper awaits, Sire, and my lord Thomas has just returned home and bade me find you.'

'Then go, and tell them we come.'

The man disappeared. With a rueful smile Henry draped his cloak about Mary's shoulders and took her arm.

'Sir Thomas is not aware of the treachery he just has committed to his liege Lord,' he commented. 'Such a tireless worker on my behalf would be saddened to know how he has thwarted me. But not for long. I shall come to you, Mary of the moonlight, with your bewitching face and moon-silver hair, and then we shall savour all the delights of love together.'

Mary was too choked with disappointment to reply. Her blood had roared in her veins, crying out for this man, only to be cheated so rudely. She looked up at his clearcut profile and sighed deeply. No matter, he had said he would come to her again, and Henry was not a man to be cheated of what he desired.

Sir Thomas was pacing up and down the great hall in agitation when Henry and Mary returned. From the stricken face of Lady Beth it was evident he had been interrogating her sharply as to her entertainment of the sovereign. Sir Thomas came eagerly to greet the King, bowing deeply, then raising bright, excited eyes to scan his face.

'Sire, you do me great honour to visit my home. I hope my lady-wife has done all in her limited power to make you comfortable.'

Henry inclined his head, his blue eyes flickering thoughtfully over his intrusive ambassador. 'In truth my lady and your daughter have been most agreeably hospitable, Thomas. I shall enjoy my stay in Kent, I think.'

At the mention of his daughter's name Sir Thomas' gaze strayed to Mary, standing meekly in the background. Something in his shrewd, narrowed eyes made Mary blush. Little escaped Sir Thomas. Was it possible he had already guessed the King's intention so far as she was concerned? As a trusted servant of King Henry it behoved Thomas to understand more than the King actually put into words on occasion, and diplomatically to carry out his lord's wishes.

'Then rest assured, Sire,' Thomas' voice continued unctuously, 'that we shall all endeavour to make your stay as happy as we may. Make free of my home, Sire, order what you will, for Your Grace is welcome to aught that is mine.'

Bowing the King to the table where supper lay ready, Sir Thomas's sapient gaze rested disconcertingly on Mary as she passed. He knew, she was certain of it now, and already his perspicacious mind was calculating the prospects.

CHAPTER TWELVE

GLISSANDO

AFTER supper Lady Beth begged Mary to go fetch her lute to entertain His Grace. Seated on a low stool in the firelight, singing as she played, Mary looked infinitely appealing and innocent, her father reflected and the King's eyes too seemed to register the same thought. Despite her silliness she could advance them all, herself, George and her father, if she took advantage of the opportunity now being offered her. He must speak to her about it as soon as the chance arose.

The ladies were the first to retire to bed, the King saying he would linger a little longer for a final draught of wine. Sir Thomas intercepted Mary in the passage way.

'Mary,' he commanded sharply, 'I want you to take great care that you please His Grace well, you understand me? See that he is frustrated from naught he desires. I wish him to be well contented here, for there is profit in it for us — all of us — if the opportunity is neatly seized. Do you catch my drift, Mary?'

She nodded, her gaze directed at the floor. Then the blue eyes came up and looked directly at him. 'You would I should bed with the King if he desires it, is that not so, Father? Then let me hasten to assure you that obedience to you has always been my aim.'

'Tush, child,' her father exclaimed irritably. 'I am not ordering you to surrender yourself like some wanton.' He hesitated, unsure how to continue, for in truth that was just what he was directing her to do. Mary saved him further embarrassment by interrupting.

'Then let me say, Father, that for once obedience to your wishes coincides with my own inclination. If His Grace desires me, I am content.'

She turned and was gone, leaving Sir Thomas open-mouthed in surprise. Diplomat that he was, accustomed to wrapping truths in polished phrases, he was startled by her outspoken words. For a well-bred maid of twenty to declare openly her willingness to sleep with a man, even a King, who most disconcerting but then Mary was renowned for her simple, shallow thinking. She had been far easier to persuade than he had anticipated. Now if it had been Anne . . .

Satisfied, Sir Thomas returned to the King.

'More wine, Sire?'

His Grace yawned widely and shook his head. 'I fear the fresh air today has quite exhausted me, Thomas, and I am ready for bed. Would you light the way?'

'Gladly, Sire,' Sir Thomas took up a candle and led the King up the staircase. 'Is there aught else Your Grace requires?' he asked as they crossed the gallery. 'The disposition of the chambers, perhaps? This door is my bedchamber, that my daughter Mary's and this yours. Servants will be within call should you wish aught.'

'Send them all to bed,' the King commanded. 'I have now all I need for the night.'

'As Your Grace wishes,' Sir Thomas replied smoothly. He stood patiently, awaiting the royal dismissal before retiring, but the King hovered hesitantly in the doorway.

'Tell me, Thomas,' he said thoughtfully at last, stroking his beard. 'Is your daughter an honest maid and true?

Sir Thomas's gaze slid from the King's eyes. This was an awkward question to answer. Honesty would compel him to admit the unsavoury rumours which had followed Mary from France, but at the same time might render her distasteful to Henry, Thomas knew well enough his sovereign's pride, which would have none of Francis's leavings. But if he lied, he would underestimate Henry's intelligence.

Instead he temporised.

'She is a dutiful maid, Sire, conscious of her duty and obedient in all matters. There is naught she would not do to prove her loyalty and love.'

Henry grunted at the non-committal reply and strode into the chamber, closing the door firmly behind him. Sir Thomas shrugged and entered his own room. He had done all he could now in the way of preparation. The rest was up to Mary — and the King.

Mary, bathed and scented and clad in her newest nightgown, lay tense in the big white bed and listened to the footfalls die away. The great chamber lay in darkness save for the shaft of silver moonlight that entered through the uncurtained window and fell athwart her counterpane, lighting the intervening floor and the silken rug. Soon it would happen, soon she and Henry would meet, not illicitly as in the wood, but with her father's blessing. Movements outside the door made her sit upright, alert and breathless.

A figure stood there, but even in the silence she knew it was he, for the great shape that towered to the lintel and whose breadth filled the doorway from side to side was not Sir Thomas.

'Mary.' The King's low, resonant voice filled the room. Mary slithered from the bed and crossed to meet him, arms outstretched. In the shaft of moonlight their shadows met and merged, and in moments Mary's nightgown was unclasped and fell silently to the floor.

'Mary, oh Mary,' the King's voice moaned softly, 'so long I have wanted you, and so long I have held back.' Between kisses, throbbing with passionate desire, he stood back to behold her, his fingertips caressing her skin. 'I swear, Mistress Mary, you have plundered your colours from the moon. White silk is your hair,' he murmured, his fingers travelling down the smooth cascade to her shoulders, 'like pearl your skin, and your eyes are moonlit pools.' Mary trembled in happiness, his touch evoking in her the wildest sensations she had ever experienced, and when he lifted her effortlessly and carried her to the great canopied bed, she was on the point of swooning in sheer delight.

Swiftly and expertly he took her, wasting no further time in verbal wooing. It was only when he lay back, breathing deeply in contentment, that he spoke again. 'Sweet Mary, scented like a rose, you are all a man dreams of in a woman.'

She snuggled closer, sighing happily. 'I am glad, my lord.'

'No cares, no worries pursue me here, Mary. In your arms I find peace.' His arm tightened about her shoulders and Mary smiled dreamily. 'There are many cares for a King, you know that, sweetheart? Pressures on me from all sides, from my courtiers and ministers, from foreign Kings and from every quarter. When it is not Wolsey who persuades and reasons, then it is my Queen or King Francis. Always there are decisions to be made, people to fight or placate. But with you, sweet Mary, I can be myself, can I not?'

'That is all I desire, Sire. Yourself.'

'And I you , sweeting.' He propped himself on his elbow to gaze at her, illuminated by the moon's rays, and surveyed her thoughtfully. 'Mary,' he said at last, 'have you ever made love by moonlight before this?'

Mary was startled by the question. It implied he knew she was no virgin, but she hestiated to admit it. Had her manner perhaps denoted past experience? He was staring thoughtfully, his finger caressing her cheek, his eyes searching and curious. Innate honesty prevailed.

'No, my lord. By candlelight and by firelight, but never by the light of the moon before now.'

A satisfied smile curved his lips. 'Then I shall call you my Mistress of the Moonlight, gentle Mary, with your pale, pearly beauty. A pearl, that is it! I shall find for you the finest pearl in my kingdom, and lay it about your sweet neck so that it may gain added lustre from your skin. This I promise you, Mary. As soon as we return to London you shall have the pearl, as a token of my love and esteem.'

She laid a finger to his lips. 'No pearl, dear my lord. No jewels, no promises, only your love, I beg.' And before he could protest she began to woo him again with the arts she had learned so well from Francis. Henry responded with delight and this time when he took her it was a slower, subtler encounter, laden with the rapture that practised finesse provokes.

Afterwards he slept, deeply and contentedly. Mary, however lay wide awake in his arms and wondered at the ecstasy the night had brought her, somehow infinitely more satisfying than love with Francis or Raoul had ever been. She smiled tenderly at Henry's sleeping face, strong yet vulnurable in slumber, and felt a rush of emotion such as she had never known, a yearning to protect and soothe, to calm and satisfy.

Just before dawn he awoke, clinging close to her, his hard athletic body so comforting against her own. At last he kissed her honey hair, his eyes moist with grateful tears, and rose to return to his own chamber. The great bed yawned emptily without him. Mary rolled over and surveyed the hollowed pillow where his head had lain, smiling wistfully. Hitherto the bed had held a virginal air, witness only to the secrets she and Anne had used to share within its downy depths so long ago, but now it had a conspiratorial atmosphere. Mary chuckled. Only it and she and Henry — oh, and Father too — hugged the secret that brought her such delight. She was the King's mistress, his chosen companion of the night! She lay in the half-light of dawn savouring the delicious title he had conferred upon her — Mistress of the Moonlight. Dear Henry! Like herself he was a romantic, a soul who yearned for undemanding love. And he should have it, she deter-

mined. Never, so long as he loved her, should she take
aught from him in return for her favours, for it was he
who conferred favour upon her, giving her his love.

Pattering footsteps and the clatter of dishes below indicated at last that the household was astir. Mary rose,
washed and dressed, and descended to the hall. Only Lady
Beth sat at table.

'Is His Grace still sleeping?' Mary enquired of her.

'Gracious no. He has been up and abroad since dawn. He
walks out in the park with your father before he breaks
his fast. Do you sit and eat with me, Mary.'

Lady Beth pushed towards her the platter of cold meat
and poured out ale into a pewter tankard. Mary sat, but
could only toy with the meat on her plate until at last
the door opened and, fresh and gusty as a breeze, Henry
strode in, his cheeks aflame and his eyes as bright and
clear as if he had slept the night through undisturbed.

Sir Thomas glided forward from behind his sovereign.
'Come now, Your Grace. I'll wager you have an appetite
now to do justice to my poor table. Pray be seated here,
Sire, betwixt my gracious wife and daughter.'

He clapped his hands loudly, then seated himself, smiling broadly. Lady Beth was scanning the King's face
closely.

'I trust you slept well, Your Grace?'

Henry nodded, his mouth full with beef. Swallowing it
noisily, he leaned over to the old lady.

'As sound and sweetly as a babe, mistress.'

Lady Beth's anxious expression softened at once into
relief. 'Then I am gratified, Sire. I made the mattress
myself, you know, of our very own finest duck feathers
and down. I am happy if you found it comfortable.'

Mary caught Henry's glance, mischievous as a child's, and
returned him an equally merry look. The same thought was
undoubtedly in both their minds — that Lady Boleyn would
indeed be agitated if she knew what antics had lately

taken place on her handiwork.

Breakfast over, the King declared his intention to spend so fine a day once more in the field, and with a blast of hunting-horns he was gone. Mary strolled in the gardens enjoying the blissful April sunshine, the heat and torpor of yesterday's thunderstorm completely vanished. Suddenly Sir Thomas appeared.

'Did the King come to you last night?'

'Yes, Father.'

'Ah.' Sir Thomas's satisfaction was evident in his sigh. 'It was apparent His Grace was well content this morning. I am glad. I trust you will continue to keep him contented, Mary, for much may come of it.' Sir Thomas's grey eyes narrowed in his angular face, making Mary think suddenly of a ferret. 'Did he say aught of recompense, of reward? Did he offer you aught, child?'

Mary thought of the pearl and blushed. Sir Thomas would be furious to know she had rejected it. 'No, Father.'

Her father walked alongside her for a few paces, deep in thought. 'Perhaps it is a little early. We must be patient and you, Mary, must continue to bring him pleasure. In time he will recollect, for he is a man of generous spirit when he is well-pleased.'

Another thought had occurred to Mary. 'Father, what will happen if I conceive his child?' she asked, her blue eyes direct and uncompromising. Sir Thomas cleared his throat.

'Therein lies no problem, daughter, for has not the precedent already been set?'

Mary recalled it, the unfortunate Bess Blount, pensioned off and languishing in Jericho. 'But is Bess happy, Father?'

'The Lady Taillebois is well provided for, and her son is to be made Duke of Richmond and taken to the Court when he is old enough. We could have worse fortune than to beget royal blood, Mary. I would relish a ducal grandson though I am but a knight, as yet. And you would not fare badly. King Henry is conscious always of his obligations.'

Obligations. Mary shuddered at the cold word. She wanted none of Henry's obligation, but his love. For love of him she would bear his child gladly, and she almost hated her callous, calculating Father for thinking only in narrow terms of duty and obligation — and reward.

'Moreover,' Sir Thomas continued ponderously. 'the mistress of a King is always regarded in high esteem, more so even than the Queen, for her influence is the greater. You must take a care, when you return to London, for many will try to use you. Pick your companions with care, Mary, for many a smiling face will conceal a scheming sycophant.'

Abruptly he turned and left her. Mary stood in the dappled shadow of a beech tree and pondered over his words. Somehow she had not thought of Henry and herself in the hotbed atmosphere of Court, but only here in the calm, unhurried air of Hever. It would be difficult at Greenwich, not only to cope with the problems Sir Thomas had just pointed out, but also to behave discreetly so that the Queen should not come to hear of Henry's liaison and be offended.

For a moment Mary felt contrite when she thought of her mistress. Stern and exacting as she was, Queen Catherine was nonetheless honest and highly respected. The last thing Mary wanted to do was to hurt her, but only to comfort and love Henry and experience his love in return. Surely she would not thus be robbing the Queen? Surely Henry had enough love in his heart for them both? For it was evident he did still care for his queen, ageing and thickening as she was. Mary calculated quickly. Henry was nearing thirty, and the Queen some seven or eight years older. Approaching forty it was to be expected that she could not still offer Henry the firm young flesh of a twenty-year-old, her body exhausted as it was from frequent harrowing pregnancies that came to naught.

The April sunlight, obscured for a moment by a passing cloud, re-emerged brilliantly to light the gravel path she walked between the high hedges of yew, and with it Mary's naturally sunny nature reasserted itself. What purpose in worrying unnecessarily about a problem not yet realised? Henry still had another day more in Hever, and what was to befall later was accordingly a problem to ponder later.

The King returned from his day's hunting in high good humour for the sport had been excellent, and Mary marvelled at his inexhaustible energy when he stole silently to her chamber again in the night hours. They lay at last in the blissful lassitude that follows love, listening to the song of the nightingale in the woods.

'I shall have you close by me in Greenwich when we return,' he murmured drowsily. Mary recalled her qualms about the Queen.

'Have no fear, I shall install you in apartments in the palace where I can reach you with ease and secretly,' he replied confidently. 'It shall be a place of luxury, with silken sheets and damask and tapestries such as you will choose for our nest,' he promised.

'You are generous, Henry, but I prefer simple things,' Mary replied softly.

'Simplicity for a sweet simple maid,' he chuckled. 'Oh Mary, I love your simplicity. So be it. We shall make love simply – in the fields, if you will, *au nature* like the nightingales. I have it, May Day! We shall lead the youths and maidens out maying in the woods, you and I, and then we shall love al fresco as I promised. Would you like that, Mall?'

It was the first time he had used this familiar form of her name, and Mary hugged the delicious sound to her. Henry rubbed his beard against her forehead.

'When do you return to London, Mary?'

'Two days after you, Sire. Her Grace gave me leave to spend a week at home.'

'Then by the time you come your chambers will be ready.'

'And the Queen? How shall I explain to her?'

'I shall give her reasons, for you, pretty sweeting, are far too transparent to plead a convincing tale.'

After a final embrace he left her, and to Mary the last day of his sojourn was interminable until he returned, exhilarated and joyful, from the hunt to take her in his arms again.

'Hasten back to Greenwich, sweetheart,' he whispered urgently in her ear as twittering birds warned of the coming dawn. 'Our idyll has been all too brief. Hasten back to my arms swiftly, for I shall languish until I hold you again.'

And suddenly he was gone, scurrying servants and clattering hoof-beats along the road the final evidence of his visit, apart from a radiant Lady Beth who, for once in her lifetime, received the accolade of congratulation from her husband on her conduct.

CHAPTER THIRTEEN

SERENADE

THE few remaining days that Mary spent at Hever seemed hollow and meaningless without Henry. Lady Beth clucked anxiously over her stepdaughter's poor appetite and wan expression.

'What ails thee, child?' Are you sure you are well enough to return to London?'

Sir Thomas threw his daughter an annoyed, contemptuous look. He had no time for all these female vapours. All the wench had had to do was to entertain the King, and here she was acting like some lovesick milkmaid. The thought amused him.

'Have you lost your tongue, mistress — or your heart? Your mother asks what ails you. You know, wife, I do believe the silly wench has lost her heart to our young and comely King!

Lady Beth clicked her tongue in deprecation, but forebore to comment what a stupid idea she considered it. Sir Thomas's eyes gleamed maliciously.

'Indeed, I do declare the maid is smitten. See how she hangs her head and sighs? Come now, Mary, half the maids at Court are no doubt besotted by His Grace's strength and manliness, but there is no need for you to do likewise.'

To his surprise Mary rose suddenly and left the hall, her face taut and lips compressed. Lady Beth watched her in alarm, and rose to follow. Sir Thomas restrained her.

'Leave her be, wife. She will come to her senses soon enough. I shall speak to her about it.'

And he did, as he and his subdued daughter rode back

towards London.

'You were asked to entertain the King, Mary, not to fall in love with him. There you overstepped the bounds of duty. Love is foolish, sentimental and unreasoning, and we can spare no room for sentiment in this business. How can we hope to make capital from the venture if you foolishly allow yourself to become infatuated with the King? It is unthinkable! I order you at once to forget it, Mary, and try to behave more shrewdly.'

Mary let his irate words flow over her unheeded. How like her father, merchant-minded as Anne had once commented, to speak of making capital out of a man's need. And Henry *was* in need of her, she was convinced of it. Her father's urgent words had as much effect on her determination to comfort Henry as a feather would on marble.

When they arrived at Placentia Mary found Henry had indeed done as he had promised, and fresh apartments were ready for her use. Attending on the Queen she expected some comment, but Queen Catherine simply enquired whether she felt refreshed after her country sojourn, commended her on her glowing appearance and sent her about her duties. Mary breathed a deep sigh of relief. Either the Queen guessed naught, or if she did she was turning a dutifully blind eye to her husband's amusements.

George Boleyn accosted Mary genially. 'I have been appointed Gentleman of the King's Bedchamber, sister, along with cousin Tom Wyatt. His Grace says he is so fond of music and song that he has a desire to have me and my lute and Tom with his poems always about him. It is a pleasant task, to be sure, to look after His Grace's fine raiment and horses and for the remainder of the time to sing and play.'

'I am glad you are so honoured, George,' Mary smiled.

George nudged her teasingly. 'I understand I am indebted to you, little sister. My thanks and eternal gratitude.'

He swept her a low, mocking bow. Mary regarded him wide-eyed. 'Me, brother? I have sought no favours for you. I do not know what you mean.'

George closed one dark eye, the other sparkling merrily. 'Our father tells me otherwise, Mary. He says all of benefit which comes to the Boleyns henceforth will be the result of your — manipulations.'

Chuckling, he left her. Mary, filled with embarrassment, went about her duties, hoping that the situation which apparently tickled George's sense of humour was not yet general gossip about the palace.

But if discretion was her intention, it did not appear to be the King's. He arrived at her apartments late that evening, singing as he came and bawling to his gentlemen to leave him now as he would have no further need of their services. Mary distinctly heard George's ribald laughter as their footsteps retreated.

Once inside the chamber he threw off his robe and strode towards her, gripping her shoulders tightly with his strong hands. His excellent spirits were evident in the sparkling eyes and curving smile.

'Mary, my love, are you not glad to see me again?'

'Indeed, my lord, I am overjoyed.'

As she spoke her fingers deftly unlaced his doublet, and Henry chuckled in delight.

'So sweet, so naive and direct! You are a treasure among women, Mall, with your gentle voice and silken body. Come to my arms, my sweeting, for I have missed you sorely.'

Candlelight accompanied their reunion this night, for the moon failed to shine. But by dawn's light Henry's gaze roved over Mary's rounded cheeks appreciatively.

'You are indeed a bewitching maid, Mall. 'Tis a pity Sir Thomas bred no more pearls such as you, for my Court shows a remarkable want of beauty.'

'But he did, Sire. I have a sister, Anne, who they say is very like me in feature.'

Henry frowned, puzzled. 'Anne? I recall no other daughter. Has my trusting Thomas kept me in ignorance of her then?'

Mary laughed. 'You met her once, though you would scarce recall it. Anne travelled with me when I attended your sister, the Princess Mary Rose, to France.'

Henry's handsome face contorted in the candlelight in his effort to recall, then suddenly smoothed. 'I have it, a little dark thing, swarthy almost and skinny as a reed. No, she has not your beauty, Mall, too thin and angular for my taste.'

'She is a woman grown now, Sire, almost eighteen and the toast of the French Court I am told. Your memory plays you somewhat false over the years, to be sure, for she is not swarthy. Black-haired, yes, and a skin like cream and the greatest black eyes like sunburnt almonds.'

Henry smiled, amused at her evident admiration for her absent sister. 'It seems time has dimmed your memory too, sweeting. Nonetheless yours is the style of beauty I prefer, all softness and warmth and plump silk fairness.' And to prove it he took her in his arms once more before he had to leave.

It was a contented King who left Mistress Boleyn's apartments at cockcrow. She was a warm and willing mistress, there was no doubt of it, as passionate and responsive a wench as any man could wish. And so unselfish, it was incredible. Not a token would she accept for her favours, not a jewel nor a house nor even a puppy. It was a pity really, because he felt so pleased with her he would have been glad to express his appreciation in some way. His mind roved quickly over the possibilities. A manor was out of the question; Mary would certainly refuse it, and in any event it would bring his current liasion ro Catherine's attention, just as she had learnt about his gift of Jericho to Bess Blount. A title would be equally flamboyant and revealing. No, he must think of some subtler and less obvious means to requite the girl.

Her father, that was it! Sir Thomas would undeniably be far less difficult to persuade to accept recompense. Not money, of course, for that would make the man appear a pandar, a procurer of his own child for the King's pleasure. But a position of some importance in the royal household, perhaps, or a minor title such as viscount. That would please the smooth-tongued creature, fawning lackey that he was.

Henry smiled happily at the solution. Well aware as he was of Sir Thomas's sycophancy, he liked him nonetheless, for the Boleyns were but newly risen like his own family and thus did not regard him as a Tudor upstart as did many of the old-established noble families. Aware of their plebeian origins, the Boleyns were lively and ambitious, father and son, and Henry enjoyed their company for they were always admiring and anxious to please.

The Queen was reading Latin with his little daughter when he reached their private apartments. Henry listened and felt pride in the clever child's accomplishment and his wife's patience and love. He surveyed the Queen's bent head appreciatively. She had not been a bad wife to him over the ten years of their marriage, and but for her failure to produce a living son he might well have been still content to share his bed only with her.

But she had given him no son. The last attempt had been yet another stillbirth and the years of hope left to her now were pitifully few. Still, he would do his duty. Two or three nights he would spend in the conjugal bed, and then the next he would indulge his pleasure with Mary. Thus he would still be vigorous in England's defence, attempting to beget an heir, yet it would still leave him time for diversion.

Wolsey would have to be handled delicately, of course, for Henry's cool-brained, clever Chancellor did not approve of his master wasting his thoughts or his energy upon a mistress. Sometimes my lord Archbishop was a trifle dictatorial, considering that he himself lived as regally as his master in his sumptuous York House, with his paramour Mistress Lark to enliven his clerical life. Yet

Henry preferred not to anger him. Wolsey, with his shrewd wits and analytical brain, was indispensable to the King. His was the mind that contrived the delicate balance of power that must be maintained between King Francis and the Emperor Charles; he it was who gave Henry the opportunity to emerge as the brilliant diplomatist who controlled the balance. The matter of the King's dalliance with Mistress Boleyn must be brought to his notice discreetly.

But spring was showering London with spasmodic rainfall and the benison of sunlight, and Henry felt the surge of spring in his veins. May Day was fast approaching, and the prospect of going Maying with the buxom, wanton Mary was too delightful to resist.

Fortune favoured Henry, for on the last day of April Wolsey appeared to be fully engaged on some private business of his own and was not there to see his King leading Mary, both clad in traditional green, as they rode out from Greenwich. Long after they had lost sight of the crowd of young knights and maidens who had accompanied them into the depths of the forest, after the glimmer of the last torch light had faded among the trees, Henry enfolded Mary in his arms. Her shimmering green gown slithered to her feet, and her lissom body quivered in his arms.

'Are you cold my love?'

'A little, my lord,' she answered tremulously.

'Then come, let me kindle the fire of love to warm us both,' he murmured tenderly, and beneath his fur-lined mantle they lay, intertwined.

In the early dawn they lingered for a last embrace before returning to the clearing where the others were already gathering boughs of young green foliage. Henry swung Mary lightly up into the saddle of her horse which an ostler held ready, then gallantly broke off a branch of hawthorn blossom to offer her.

'You must not return empty-handed, sweeting, for maying was the reason for our venture,' he quipped and with a gay smile he too swung himself into the saddle, then side by side they rode home.

If the Queen saw or heard of her going into the woods with the King, she made no mention of it to Mary. In her manner towards her lady-in-waiting Mary could detect no change at all; she was as polite and charming as ever.

Spring blossomed into summer and life at the King's Court never relaxed for an instant. Feasting and jousting, dancing, games and constant entertainment excited Mary's spirits until she felt fatigued, only to be revived again by Henry's constant attention and ardent lovemaking. Occasionally the Queen bore her husband company at a masked ball or tournament, only to retire early, exhausted. Some said it was the King's untiring exuberance she could not match; others whispered that she was once again with child. Whatever the reason, the Queen's withdrawal left Henry free to enjoy Mary's company all the more, and it was evident he took pleasure in seeing the wonder-filled admiration in her wide eyes.

'For six hours you have played tennis, my lord,' she would breathe incredulously, 'and still you do not need to pause for breath. I marvel at Your Grace's strength and stamina.'

Or, again, 'Seven men you have unhorsed in the jousting today, Sire, and not one man amongst them has the power even to shake you in the saddle.'

It gave her infinite pleasure to watch his virile body, bursting with vitality as he indulged his favourite pastimes, and to know that still he would come to her at night. He was proud of his strength and athletic skill, and only once did he speak of the future and the fears it held for him.

'I grow old, Mall,' he murmured into her silken hair. 'Soon I shall be thirty, and my strength will fade. What joy is there in life for an old man, grey-haired and enfeebled? I would I could stop time and stay young forever.'

Mary cradled his head in her arm. 'You are yet young, my lord, and have yet some years to go before you reach your full prime. But if the day's jousting has sapped your vigour, then sleep now and refresh yourself,' she murmured soothingly. Henry stiffened.

'Sapped my vigour? I have yet the vigour of ten men, as you shall see,' he said abruptly, and took her swiftly in his arms.

Then came the sultry night Henry came to Mary's chambers, not with the eager gait of a lover, but with the shambling, melancholy air of one wrapped in introspection.

'Mary, I am unwell,' he complained as she divested him of his doublet, guiding him into a chair and easing off his boots. 'My head aches, and there is a strange uneasiness in my bowels. Think you I have been poisoned?' He sat up abruptly at the unpleasant notion. Mary soothed him, her fingertips caressing his aching brow.

'No, Sire. You are well-loved by all.'

'But inadvertently, perchance. Have you seen those verminous creatures that pass for scullions in my kitchens? Greasy, unkempt, filthy creatures all!'

'Then come to bed, Sire, and sleep will banish all pain. By morning you will be well again.' Mary reached for his points, anxious to undress him and draw him into the intimate darkness of the curtained bed. Henry's hands clutched her fingers irritably, staying her.

'I am ill I tell you, wench. Go fetch Tom Wyatt and your brother George to help me to my bed, then they must summon the physician. Oh! the pain in my head!' He clutched his brow, his eyes widening. 'See, Mary! Feel how I sweat!'

Indeed he was hot, Mary had to agree. Reluctantly she summoned George and Tom, who bore their moaning master away. Mary could see the fear in Henry's dilated eyes as he stumbled between the two younger men, and he said not a word to Mary before he left.

CHAPTER FOURTEEN

DISSONANCE

FOR three days Henry tossed helplessly on his bed, wrack-
ed with pain and sweating feverishly. Mary, despite her
duties to the Queen, hovered anxiously awaiting a summons to him, but none came.

'He is too ill and convinced his is close to death,'
George Boleyn told her.

'But he is not like to die!' Mary cried, alarmed at
the prospect. She had not realised till this moment
how dear he was to her, this powerful, vulnerable monarch
of England, with all his failings.

'Not he.' George's voice was calmly reassuring. 'He has
the strength of a bull, and many before him have survived
the sweating sickness. The physicians say he will live,
and Wolsey sits constantly at his bedside exhorting and
encouraging. It is more than any man dare do, to die if
Wolsey forbids it!'

Despite the danger, George could joke, so Henry could
not be dying, Mary reasoned. But the mere possibility of
his death frightened her. Since mother died there had
been no one to hold any permanent place in her heart
but Henry. Surely God could not be so cruel as to rob
her of him too?

Henry did not die. The fourth day he reappeared, still
a little unsure in his gait, but the following day he emerged brisk and energetic. Just as suddenly as the sickness
had smitten, so rapidly did he throw it off. Mary, rejoicing
in his recovery, awaited his coming impatiently. It was
only then, as she hovered hopefully in the corridor for

Henry to pass, that she became aware of the flitting shadow of a man.

She turned quickly, curious as to the identity of the shadow which, now she came to think of it, had been lurking nearby throughout the three days of Henry's distress, and caught sight of a fair-haired page who slipped quietly away. But she quickly forgot him as Henry's distant laughter could be heard and he turned the corner towards her. Mary's eager smile faded swiftly when she saw that he held the Queen's elbow attentively, his russet head inclined towards hers as they passed, deep in conversation.

Neither the fourth nor the fifth day did Henry come to her and Mary languished, sorrowful at his neglect. Once more she became aware of the pale-haired page who seemed always to hover behind her at a discreet distance, watching all she did, but far enough removed to render question impossible. It was as Mary strolled in the castle gardens that curiosity finally overwhelmed her when she spotted him yet again, and deliberately loosening the gilt pomander from her girdle, she let it fall to the ground as if unheeded. Instantly he darted forward to retrieve it and presented it to her with a bow.

'My thanks, sir,' Mary smiled sweetly. 'I do not think I know you, for we have never met. How are you named, sir?'

'Will Carey, mistress, and your humble servant,' Again he bowed, and as he straightened Mary could see that he was indeed a handsome youth, some two or three years older than herself, with a kindly curve to his mouth and liquid brown eyes that reminded her of Lady Beth's favourite spaniel.

'I do not remember seeing you before, Will Carey. What are your duties at the Court?' she enquired.

'I am a page to the Queen, ma'am, no one of consequence. As the younger son of a very minor country gentleman, there is no reason why you should notice me,' he countered, his youthful face tinged pinkly in embarrassment.

Mary instantly felt sorry for him; she too knew the discomfort of feeling out of place amongst richer, cleverer folk. Smiling again to put him at his ease, she walked on as she spoke, obliging him to fall in step beside her.

'I spoke less than the truth, Will, for I confess I have noticed you before. What maid would not take note of a comely young man?' she laughed, then seeing his sombre expression did not soften, she went on. 'I have seen you oftimes, close to me yet not near enough to speak. I have noticed how silently and unobtrusively you follow me. Why is that, Will Carey? Have you no troth-plight of your own to pursue?'

She cocked her fair head to one side, but Will's gaze dropped sheepishly and he did not answer. 'Answer me, Will. Are there not many pretty wenches about the Court? Surely one amongst them takes your fancy?'

The dark eyes leapt to meet her gaze, direct and uncompromising. 'There are many such, mistress, but none so beautiful as you,' he blurted out. 'Forgive me — I know no courtly speech. I can only say what is in my mind, Mistress Mary. I want always to be close to you, watching over you, and I have seen how sorrowful you have been of late. If there is aught I can do . . .'

He hung his head again miserably, his hands interlocked, clenched. Mary noted how supple and powerful the hands appeared as she turned over in her mind what he was saying, then suddenly he cast one final glance at her, a look full of mute adoration such as the spaniel's, and fled.

Still Henry did not come, though by the vigorous manner in which he now played tennis and danced it was evident that he was fully recovered. Mary sighed, feeling a little forlorn and forgotten, and waited with hope. Carey's attentive, unobtrusive presence helped to reassure her that she was not completely insignificant in this glittering Court.

Then without warning Henry suddenly appeared in her doorway one night, his face beaming and his arms outstretched. Dismissing her woman attendant, Mary went eagerly towards him.

'Forgive me my Mistress of the Moonlight,' Henry murmured as his great arms closed about her, sending shudders of happiness through her. 'Forgive me that I neglected you so long. So many affairs, you know, so much to attend to after my illness.'

Despite the words of apology there was no humility in his tone, and the confidence of his smile made it evident he believed himself already forgiven by his coming. Mary made no word of reproach; she was content that at last he had remembered her.

Sensing her capitulation, Henry whooped with delight and carried her, laughing, to the great bed. Later, relaxing with his head on her breast, he murmured of the troubles which had seethed in his brain.

'I never speak to you of state matters, Mall, for with you I have no need to dissemble or be the diplomat. With you, alone of all those I know, I can be myself. But I must tell you why I seemed indifferent of late. Far from indifference, Mall, I longed for your warmth and love, but my illness gave me cause to fear for my Crown. Wolsey believed it was witchcraft made me ill, for I have many enemies. I think mayhap he was right, and I have no son to succeed me, so as soon as I could I returned to my duty. I visited the Queen each night, Mall. It cannot be laid at my door if I beget no son.'

Mary listened, her fingers caressing his hair, but spoke no word.

'You are not angry, sweetheart, nor jealous?'

'No, Sire. It is, as you have said, your duty to your country which I know you love well. I am honoured that you have a little love for me too.'

'Dear Mall!' He cradled her closer. 'So sweet, so understanding. You are a rare woman indeed, who can comprehend the deep love I bear to England. It is a position of high responsibility, to be King of such a realm, and one I am proud to hold. Do you realise how much power I wield, Mall, balancing the power between Francis of France and Charles the Emperor? It demands a man of great dedication like myself to wield such authority — guided by such as Wolsey, of course.'

Mary nodded sleepily, though she followed little of what he meant. That he needed her in order to find peace and respite from his cares she understood well, however, and delighted in the thought.

'But come, let's talk no more of duty,' Henry whispered hoarsely in the darkness. 'Let us talk instead of love.'

In the succeeding weeks Mary found herself once again constantly close to Henry in his feverish pursuit of pleasure, dancing at masked balls, gliding contentedly in a sumptuously decorated barge along the willowed river banks, and on one occasion at a lavish feast given by Wolsey in his magnificent York House. Henry eyed the gold-liveried servants and gold and silver plate with undisguised envy, wondering at the endless succession of platters carried in and the rapt attention with which all the beautiful women regarded their fleshy-faced host.

'Is it not strange, Mall,' Henry murmured to Mary, 'how my one-time chaplain, son of a mere cattle-merchant, can aspire to such splendour, greater even than his King's? Even his house here outstrips all my palaces. I would dearly like to own York House, Mary.'

'Why, Your Grace has no need of further palaces?'

He smiled fondly. 'It would be a setting worthy of your beauty, my little pearl,' he said softly. 'And if one day I chance to procure York House, yours it shall be Mall, I promise.'

Mary smiled deprecatingly. 'I do not need it, my lord. I have no need for a permanent setting for wherever you are is my place.'

He patted her hand once again, contented at her docil-
ity, her total lack of acquisitive greed. Nevertheless,
he thought discontentedly, *he* would be glad of a reason
to persuade Wolsey to part with this superb mansion; he
would not hesitate to accept it if it were offered to him.

Henry rose with the swiftness that accompanied his
many sudden decisions. 'Come, sweetheart, let us take
the barge back to Placentia,' he said, offering his bejewelled hand to Mary. Mary rose dutifully and in turning, caught her foot against a page who pressed too
closely, and stumbled. Henry drew in his breath, swiftly,
irritated by the youth's pressing closeness.

'Out of the way, fool,' he muttered sharply, and the
fair-haired youth backed away, bowing and murmuring apology. Henry recognised him now, the ubiquitous
Carey, ever close in Mary's shadow and ever gazing at her
with the rapt intentness that could only indicate he was besotted with her. Henry smiled. It afforded him proud
satisfaction that other men, however menial, should regard his treasures with envy, and Mary was undoubtedly
a jewel of a woman. He let his gaze rest on her rounded
plumpness as she made her way from the chamber, and felt
again the lurching restlessness in his loins.

As they lay, reclining in the silk-lined barge, Henry
took her hands in his. 'Soon, my sweeting. I fear I shall
have to forgo your loving company for a time, but do not
fear.'

The round blue eyes gazed at him enquiringly but there
was no hint of reproach. He felt her hands tremble, but
did not know whether she shivered from apprehension or
the cold January night air. He drew her fur-lined cloak
closer about her.

'Wolsey has been busy on my behalf and has arranged
for the young Emperor Charles to come to London soon,
in the spring, and presently afterwards I am to go to

France, to meet with Francis. You, of course, will accompany me in the Queen's train, but we shall have little opportunity to meet. But after, Mall, in the summertime we shall relax again and enjoy each other's company. You will be patient, my pearl, will you not?'

But although Mary, acquiescent and untroubled, found contentment in her sovereign's assurances, her peace was suddenly and rudely shattered from a quarter she least anticipated. Before the month of sleet and snow had left London Mary was suddenly summoned to her mistress's prescence.

She curtseyed low, awaiting a summons to lay out a fresh shift or fetch Her Grace's missal, but Queen Catherine stood silent before the log fire, eyeing her lady-in-waiting thoughtfully before speaking. Mary watched this pale-faced woman, her sombre, old-fashioned farthingale merging into the shadows about her, and marvelled at Henry's devotion to such a plain, ageing woman.

Suddenly Catherine turned, her stiff brocade gown rustling like waves on the pebbled beach, and she faced her gentlewoman squarely.

'Mistress Boleyn, I am loth to believe ill of a maid so gentle as you, but if I am to believe what I am assured, then you have been a faithless servant to me. No,' she raised an imperious hand, 'I do not ask whether it be true for I see by your blushes that it is. Know only that I will not be betrayed. I, Queen of England, daughter of the illustrious Ferdinand and Isabella, will not be cheated by a mere country squire's wench.'

She paused, allowing her head to incline a little so as to gauge Mary's reaction, and seeing the fair head bent low, her voice softened.

'I wish you no harm, Mary Boleyn, and you need fear no revenge from me. But I would have you know that the evil ways into which my impious courtiers seek to mislead His Grace can have only evil results. I know you are not solely to blame; it is your father and your Howard kin who use you, whether you are aware of it or not. You are but an instrument, I fear, a guileless child trapped in the snares of others.

'But this I know. His Grace's marriage cannot be blessed while he lives thus in sin. Therefore I order you to see it ceases forthwith. Then, and only then, I am convinced, will our marriage be blessed with a son.'

Catherine paused and looked Mary full in the face, her dark Spanish eyes eloquent with pleading, though there was only hauteur in her words. Mary, for the first time, felt consumed with remorse and pity for her mistress.

'Go now, Mistress Boleyn, and pray as I shall do for guidance and God's blessing.' The words were barely a whisper. Catherine had asked for no promise; as Queen she expected obedience.

Shame-faced, Mary dropped a low curtsey and turned to leave. As her hand touched the doorknob the Queen's voice reached her again across the chamber.

'I think, Mistress, in order to ensure your continued good behaviour, it would be wise to arrange matters so that you put less temptation in His Grace's way.' The voice was low, contemplative. Mary hung hesitantly, wondering what was to follow.

'Methinks it would be as well if you were married, mistress.'

A gasp escaped Mary's lips before she could think. 'Married, Your Grace?' she stammered. 'But — to whom?'

'I know not yet. It is a question I must discuss with His Grace, but I doubt not he will come round to my way of thinking presently. So you had best prepare, child, and perchance you yourself may suggest a husband. Think on it, but for now, go to the chapel and pray.'

On the cold flagged floor Mary knelt, trembling with fear and shock. To be married, so suddenly, and to a husband yet unknown! It was cruel, unthinkable! To be bereft of Henry's loving embrace and thrust into the arms of another, possibly cold and unloving man! Mary wept bitter tears of shame mixed with apprehension. So long as she could remember she had been pushed into events against her will, a pawn in a game, a victim trapped in a fantasy world whether of her father or someone else's making. What was to become of her now? She had never wittingly harmed anyone in her life. All she had ever sought was love to requite her own yearning, and just as she believed she had found it with Henry, her life was to be joined, coldly and without passion, to a stranger. Mary's warm tears fell to the flagged floor, cooling rapidly in the icy air to form pearls of sorrow.

CHAPTER FIFTEEN

FUGUE

A maelsrtom of swift events suddenly seemed to encircle Mary, and dizzied by their rapidity, she simply allowed herself to be caught up in the swirling eddy and carried along. It was as it had always been. Others dictated, Mary followed unquestioningly.

A tight-faced Henry, fresh from a lengthy interview with his Queen, summoned Mary to his presence. Dismissing a wryly-smiling George among his other attendants, he bade Mary be seated then, standing with his broad back towards her, he addressed the frost-patterned window panes.

'The Queen is adamant, Mary; you are to be wed forthwith. I do not wish to upset her by refusing — though, mark you, I would not wish you to think me ruled by a woman. I could refuse her request.'

Mary sat silent, ignoring the note in his voice that invited comment. After a moment, Henry continued.

'Then all that remains is to determine your husband, it seems. Have you any preference, Mary?'

She sat dumb, bewildered by his calm acceptance. Henry turned testily to face her.

'Well, is there one you would choose?'

She shook her fair head miserably. Henry sighed.

'Then I must determine for you. Have no fear, Mall, I shall not be unkind and choose you a dry old man. He shall be young and lusty, I promise you.'

Tear-filled blue eyes rose to meet his gaze. 'Shall I see you no more, Sire?' Her tiny, terrified voice brought compassion to Henry's sombre eyes but, standing still and aloof, he answered awkwardly.

'We shall see each other about the Court, of course, for I doubt Her Grace intends to dismiss you. Now go and you shall learn presently who is to be your husband.'

Mary stared. So coolly he had accepted the fact of their parting, a sudden severance after a year in which they had lain and loved together so intimately. Numb with misery and disbelief she rose and left him.

From the window Henry could see her crossing the courtyard below, her golden head bowed in grief, and remorse gnawed his guts. Remorse at his casual dismissal of the faithful wench mingled with regret, for he was loth to be forced to abjure her unstinted caresses. Damn Catherine for turning capricious like this! Usually she was sensible enough to turn a blind eye to his amorous activities. The thought crossed his mind that perchance Catherine was yet again with child, for it was usually only then that she took such whims into her head. In that case, it was better not to cross her, more especially so just now when negotiations were so advanced for him to meet her Emperor-nephew, Charles, for who could tell how great her influence might be with him?

A cloaked figure emerged from the cloisters below in the courtyard and hastened to follow Mary's retreating figure. Henry's plump face creased into a smile. Of course! Will Carey, the love-smitten page who mutely adored Mary Boleyn — he would make her the perfect husband!

Henry slapped his great thigh in contentment. Now if only Catherine would agree to it, his problems would be ended. Will Carey would make a devoted husband, solicitous and kind, yet ever-understanding, Henry felt sure. Moreover his lean, boyish frame would present no rival for Henry with his fine calves and breadth of body — Mary would still yearn for him. The young colt Carey would never satisfy her animal passions, and her arms would still reach longingly for Henry's virile presence. Yes, that was the answer! After all, Henry himself was doomed to an uxorious life for which he was never destined; of what use to him was a monogamous marriage? To him, blessed with the stamina to satisfy a stable full of women?

Henry dined with a hearty appetite before going to consult with his Queen. Catherine, as was ever her manner, listened in silence and digested his words thoughtfully before answering.

'Will Carey? He is but a page, Sire, and a younger son with no expectations. I doubt your Thomas Boleyn will be well pleased at the match,' she commented soberly at last.

'Thomas? He is away in France on my business and is not here to be consulted, Madam. But he is not like to be offended at the matching of his daughter to one who is kinsman to the King. Carey too is descended from the Beauforts like myself.'

'But a page nonetheless, Henry.'

'Then I shall appoint him Gentleman to the Privy Chamber, equal to George Boleyn. That should satisfy Thomas.'

'Then so be it. Is Will Carey agreeable?'

Henry cleared his throat. 'I have yet to speak to him of the matter, but he will be agreeable — delighted, if I am not mistaken.'

Catherine nodded. 'Then let the marriage proceed forthwith. I myself shall attend the ceremony to preclude any evil rumour.'

Poor Will Carey could hardly believe his ears when his sovereign, summoning him to the Great Chamber, bade him wed the voluptuous Mistress Boleyn forthwith. Stunned, overjoyed and bereft of speech, he stood blank-faced before the King.

'Well, man?' Henry demanded irritably. 'You love her, do you not?'

Will hung his head shame-facedly. It seemed nigh on treachery to admit to loving the King's mistress.

'Answer me, man! You love her and wish to serve her, do you not?'

'I do, Sire, and will serve her as faithfully as I do Your Grace.'

Henry dismissed him, satisfied with the fool's answer. Carey was an insignificant creature, anxious to please his master in any way. Flattered by having a beauteous creature like Mary to wife, he would put no obstacle in the way of the King's desires. It had been a clever after-thought to promote the fellow to be a Gentleman of the Privy Chamber too, for if he were kept fully occupied there, his wife of necessity would not be far away, and accessible. Contentedly Henry allowed the preparations for Mary's marriage to proceed.

Mary, like a snared bird, felt powerless, seeing no way of escape that would lead to certain safety and happiness. Of all the men about the Court the King might have chosen, Will Carey was probably the least obnoxious, and he certainly seemed to care for her.

In the dim grey light of a February morning she raised her eyes to steal a surreptitious glimpse of him as he stood beside her at the altar in Greenwich Chapel. Dark lashes lay across his cheeks, obscuring the clear brown eyes as he listened to the priest's words. Mary glanced quickly at Henry, standing close with Queen Catherine, but he kept his gaze averted. George, the only other member of the Boleyn family present, stood erect and tight-lipped behind the King. Queen Catherine, pale and composed, fingered her rosary beads until the moment came for her to move forward to make the customary offerings at the altar. That done, she withdrew to stand again at Henry's side, regal and aloof. The bride watched every movement about her as though in a dream; nothing in this chill, gloom-shrouded chapel had a semblance of reality about it, neither the ethereally pale figures surrounding her nor the strange numbness within her.

And then suddenly it was all over. The wedding feast concluded, all the actors in this unreal mummery vanished from the scene, leaving her alone in a nightshift in a flower-garlanded bedchamber with Will Carey. It was strange, she mused, how one's life could shuttle one so swiftly from being mistress to a King to wife to a page — and all in the space of a few days.

'Mary,' he murmured, taking a hesitant step towards her, 'you have no need to fear me, I promise. I shall love and care for you always.'

But Mary's ears were deaf to his words. She was mesmerised by the little cloud of breath that rose from his lips and hovered in the icy air above him before dissipating swiftly into the gloom. Despite the log fire the chamber was bitterly chill. Carey's hands trembled as he embraced her unsurely and coaxed her towards the bed.

Icy skin meeting chill flesh soon melted into mutual warmth, and Mary felt again the sudden surge of pleasure that always came with ardent embracing. It mattered little that this time her lover was not of her own choosing; his solicitous concern and gently fumbling fingers aroused a warm flood of sympathy and she was anxious to please, to repay him for his kindliness. Will Carey's was not the powerful, consuming passion that she was accustomed to with Henry, a gusty, all enveloping possession with the fierce directness of an energetic bull, but a simple, sensitive winning-over that betrayed his lack of expertise. Nonetheless Mary responded warmly.

In the early light of dawn Mary smiled fondly at the tousled, sleeping head beside her, a warm, maternal feeling for her young husband pervading her. Fate could have been more cruel. With this courteous Will Carey to care for her, life would not be too harsh, even if she were to be forever deprived of Henry's love. Nonetheless a sigh of nostalgia escaped her.

Will turned over sleepily, then smiled up at her, his hand reaching for hers under the covers. 'Mary Carey, I love you,' he said softly, and closed his eyes again.

Throughout the *lune de miel,* the month of honey accorded to newly-wedded couples, no duties were expected of Mary or of Will about the Court. But by the end of February both returned to serve their King and Queen. Mary half-expected Will to repeat some chance comment of the King's regarding their marriage and how they fared, but to her secret disappointment Henry seemed to have forgotten her, for Will said naught. And though Mary still pined for Henry's caresses, by night Will endeavoured to atone for his master's default.

'His Grace grows anxious over the Emperor Charles' delay,' Will commented. 'He is eager to meet the Queen's nephew and frets that affairs in Spain delay the Emperor's coming.'

But Henry's disappointments faded into insignificance for Mary when her father suddenly arrived at Placentia, newly returned from France. Without warning he presented himself at Mary's chambers.

'What is this I hear from your brother?' he demanded savagely, all thought of greeting forgotten in his anger. 'That you are wed to some piddling page without reference to me? Explain yourself, mistress, if you can. Explain how a daughter may see fit to wed without recourse to her father?'

He stood, arms akimbo, silhouetted against the window, his face dark with rage. Mary stood meekly before him.

'It is done, Father, and by no will of mine.'

'Then how, in heaven's name?'

'The Queen demanded it, to remove me from His Grace's reach.'

'She discovered he bedded with you? Then the more fool you for your indescretion. But wedded to a page, that is intolerable! I did not believe Her Grace bore me such malice as to humiliate me thus. Was it she who chose your husband?'

'His Grace suggested Will Carey to me, and I agreed, Father, for I like him well. And he is no longer page, but Gentleman to the Privy Chamber.'

'But a younger son and penniless for all that! You fool, you stupid, mindless child! Could you do no better for yourself, and you mistress to the King?'

Thomas's eyes flashed with fury as he paced angrily up and down. Then a thought struck him.

'Perchance we can annul the marriage yet on the grounds of non-consummation.'

Mary looked up, startled. 'That you cannot, Father, nor would I wish it.'

'Are you defying me girl?'

'I am married to Will Carey, and will remain so. That is all there is to be said.'

She heard the crack of Thomas's riding-whip as he brought it down against his thigh.

'I little thought that you, of all my children, would dare to cross me so, but since you prove so defiant, hear this. I shall renounce you utterly, Mary; henceforth you shall be no daughter of mine, do you hear? You may bring yourself to what degradation you will, but you shall climb by no effort of mine. The Boleyns were born to rise, and we shall, George and Anne and I, but you with your seeming simpleness were ever of an obdurate nature. Do as you will, wench, but you are no longer a Boleyn!'

He glared at her, his eyes charged with menace and venom, but Mary simply stood and looked directly back at him, uncringing and for once, unafraid.

'As you will, Father. No longer Mary Boleyn but Mary Carey,' she answered quietly, and curtseyed her indication that the conversation was ended. Thomas stared in indignant surprise for a second, then swept furiously from the room.

For the new young bride it seemed as though suddenly she could find favour with no one, save Will. Her father, busy in his affairs about the Court, would stare through her as if she no longer existed; even brother George, hitherto always affable even if a trifle mocking of his sister's mental limitations, seemed to take the cue from his father. Mary's duties to the Queen kept her constantly close to both Her Grace and to the King, but neither ventured her a smile nor even a charitable word. The studied rejection of the others Mary could accept, but Henry's cold gaze brought bitter tears to her eyes while Carey slept. As it had always been, so it still was; however she tried to please and accommodate others, she gained no loving concern in return.

Save for Will, she corrected herself. Whatever her mood, silent with sadness, or brittle with feigned gaiety, Will's smile never left his lips nor did his arms fail to encircle her with a love that was transparently unalloyed. Dear Will. She could have fared worse than find such a simple, uncomplicated love which demanded naught in return.

Henry, the King, seemed to grow visibly more and more irritable and changeable of mood, cuffing and kicking his valets and bestowing a smile on none. It was the Emperor Charles' continued delay, Will explained to Mary. Then suddenly word came that Charles had disembarked at Dover. Instantly Henry was all smiles and eagerness, impatient of further delay. The whole Court must pack instantly and accompany him to Dover to greet the Emperor instead of awaiting him at Greenwich.

Gusts of feverish preparation engulfed the Court. Mary must attend her mistress to Dover, and Will His Grace. As the journey proceeded, and Mary sat in a litter heavily draped against the May breezes, Henry drew up alongside her for a moment, bent from his horse and pulled back the curtain. Mary stared in surprise at the unexpected figure in russet velvet.

'Now matters begin to speed as I wished, little pearl,' Henry murmured softly. 'Soon we shall meet again, you and I, I promise, and I shall know again the sweet pleasures of my Mistress of the Moonlight.'

The curtain fell, and he was gone. But in Mary's breast hope fluttered again, and joy that Henry had not dismissed her from his heart for ever after all.

CHAPTER SIXTEEN

RONDO

IT was not, to Mary's intense disappointment, during the Emperor's visit that the King came again at last to her arms. Henry seemed fully occupied in ensconcing his Queen and retinue at Canterbury, in the Archbishop's Palace, so as to leave himself free to hasten onwards to Dover. And even when he returned to Canterbury with the puny, unprepossessing young Emperor beside him, he seemed too full of ebullience and eager talk with Charles to notice Mary.

It was Queen Catherine who enlightened her. 'His Grace seeks to betroth our little daughter the Princess Mary to the Emperor.' Poor little maid, thought Mary, barely four years of age and already to be plighted to this pale-eyed, stunted youth.

'One day my daughter will be Empress,' the Queen added soberly as if reading Mary's thoughts.

Then suddenly Charles rode away to visit his fleet at Sandwich and the Court was ordered to depart to Dover, ready to embark for France. Henry's next rendezvous was to be with King Francis.

The weather sprang unexpectedly into warmth, the great cavalcade showering the hedge-roses with dust as it lumbered along the rutted roads towards the coast. Occasionally Will Carey would draw up anxiously by Mary's litter to ensure she was comfortable and not overtired by the heat and choking dust.

'Thank you, Will. I am well,' she would assure him. She saw little of her husband these days, but always he was concerned for her and Mary was grateful.

The vista that spread before the English party when it arrived at last in the *Val Doré* took Mary's breath away. Never in her most fanciful dreams had she envisaged such splendour as lay before her now. On this side of the valley, near a town named Guisnes, Wolsey had had prepared a fantastic pavilion for Henry and Catherine, huge as a palace and adorned with tapestries and silks of brilliant hues. On the far side of the valley, at Ardres, the myriad colours of their French hosts could be seen against a background of silken tents and pavilions. And across the valley the two monarchs of France and England saluted each other, each resplendent in glittering silver and cloth of gold.

Mary drew in her breath sharply. Both men looked so god-like astride their horses, their plumed velvet caps surmounting handsome, haughty faces. And both men had once favoured her with their caresses. She watched with pride as each king rode down into the valley to the sound of trumpets to meet, embrace, and enter the pavilion of cloth of gold together.

The women's quarters were among the thousands of white silk tents which lay behind the golden royal pavilion, far removed from the quarters of the gentlemen. Nonetheless as Mary lay, naked on account of the still closeness of the June night, Will found occasion to sneak in to her in the darkness, and Mary found the comfort of his arms well-pleasing despite the heat.

In the morning sunlight Mary's gaze was again dazzled by the silver tissue and purple fringes decking the tents, the gilded banners and garlands of sweet-scented roses, and across the valley the silver statue of St. Michael that topped the Franch King's pavilion. Such luxury, such extravagance she had never seen! Wryly she wondered how her careful father, deliberately remote, would view this Gallic wastefulness.

Then suddenly across the sea of green turf a slight figure

came hastening, a dark-haired girl whose face shone in a welcoming smile. Mary stared as she recognised the smooth-skinned maid, elegant in vivid turquoise silk, as her sister.

'Anne! Oh Anne!' she cried, throwing her arms enthusiastically about her slender body. 'I scarcely knew you, Nan, so much you have changed!'

And so she had. From a skinny maid of thirteen, Anne had now grown to a tall, slender woman with glistening black hair, but still the same dark slanting eyes that twinkled with mischief. But so elegant! Her gown was fashionably cut and her hair dressed in a new and fetching style. And about her neck she wore a studded collar, a fashion Mary had never seen hitherto.

'You have not changed though, Mall,' Anne commented, standing back to look the better at her. 'Still as fair and plump and comely as I remember. I'd have known you anywhere. Tell me, is Father here? And George, and Tom, and Mother?'

Mary blushed. 'Father is here, and George too, and our uncle and Tom Wyatt, though I have seen them not.'

'Not? Why, Mall what is amiss?'

Anne's shrewd dark eyes searched her face, and Mary knew better than to try to deceive her. 'I am wed, Anne, to a man Father despises and therefore he scorns and rejects me. But I care not, for Will Carey is a fine man. But harken — George has his wife here too. You have not met Jane, but I warn you, she has a shrewish tongue, that one.'

'I dare swear I'll be a match for her,' Anne retorted laughing, and Mary was grateful that she quizzed no more about her marriage to Carey.

The *Val Doré* rang to the sound of thudding hooves as the great love-feast between the monarchs began with jousting and tourneys. Excitement waxed high as English and French archers and bowmen competed and drank toasts together, embracing and back-slapping and downing vast

quantities of ale while their betters emptied the casks
of malmsey and claret. Spectators cheered in the stands,
and Frenchmen and Englishmen alike swore undying affection to the sound of trumpet calls, and in the vast chapel
priests and prelates knelt with Kings and Queens to pray
for perpetual peace and amity between their nations.

It was a foetidly hot day when Mary stood watching
Henry challenging all comers to the joust. Not one could
even shake him in the saddle, and she glowed proudly
at the glorious sight of him. Anne nudged her elbow.

'Father told me.'

'Told you what, Nan?'

'That you had to be married off to Carey at the Queen's
command, because you were His Grace's mistress.'

'Are you ashamed of me, Nan?' Mary asked quietly.

Anne's light laugh denied the thought. 'Why should I
be, sister? If Will Carey is content to take his master's
leavings, why should I fret? But no, it is an honour to
bed with a king, Mall, but folly to gain naught from it.'

Her father's daughter, thought Mary sadly. She had not
thought of Anne before as grasping.

'I too would bed with a king, given the chance,' Anne
whispered confidingly. Mary looked up sharply. Her sister's
eyes gazed adoringly into the distance, and Mary followed
her gaze. It was Francis who stood, smiling at his brother-
king's exploits on horseback, unaware of Anne's meaning-
ful look.

'Francis?' Mary said in surprise.

Anne nodded, then tossed her head as though angered
at her own indiscretion. 'And I have seen your husband,
Mary. Rather a pleasant fellow, I thought, though but a
country squire.'

Mary stilled the feeling of protective resentment that
rose in her at her sister's words. After all, it was true
enough; Will was a pleasant fellow, but it seemed to damn
him through faint praise. He was more — he was sensitive;

he was kind and tender, but this Anne would never admire. For her, as for Father, kindness and gentleness had no part in life at Court, for they were signs of weakness.

During the days of feasting and jousting that followed, Francis and Henry became mutually more and more amicable as the wine flowed, kissing and embracing jovially. By the gleam in Henry's eye Mary began to hope that, in his contentment, he would come to her at last.

The same thought was lurking in Henry's wine-mused mind. He had caught sight of the full-bosomed, soft-skinned maid whose embraces he had missed for so long, and the thought of sinking blissfully between those milky breasts seemed the perfect ending to a fine day. Once Catherine was abed he would slip silently to the ladies' quarters, and he knew already which was Mary's tent.

'Come, a final goblet of wine before we retire,' said Francis, jerking Henry out of his daydream. Queen Claude, catching Queen Catherine's eye, rose to bid the gentlemen good-night. Queen Catherine followed. Francis threw an affectionate arm across Henry's shoulders.

'We are brothers, you and I, Henry, and I love you well,' Francis slurred happily.

'And I you, brother.'

'And to prove it I shall make you a gift of aught that is mine. Tell me — what shall it be, brother? My horse, my splendid black stallion? Or a fine jewel? Or,' his voice lowered to a confidential whisper, 'or one of my beautiful women — hm?'

Henry's mind was already ahead in a white silk tent with white silken arms about him. 'Thank you, no, brother. Your munificence already overwhelms me.' Francis' eyes narrowed. Henry recalled again the continual rivalry between them, the constant effort of each to outdo the other. 'But what can I offer you, in token of our friendship? A horse, a jewel, a woman? It seems you have all in abundance already.

Francis smiled, that slow, calculating smile of his that irritated Henry beyond measure. 'As you say, brother, but there is one small mark of your affection I would esteem.'

'Then name it, and it is yours,' Henry answered proudly. None could say he was not generous.

'It is but a trifling thing,' Francis murmured as he inspected his jewelled fingers. 'A maid, one of Her Grace's ladies, who takes my fancy.'

Suspicion nibbled, but Henry had given his word. 'Then name her, if you know her name, and she is yours. I have said it.'

'Her name is Mademoiselle Marie Boullan. No one of import, I believe, though I understand you have sometimes found her pleasing.'

'I did,' Henry admitted grudgingly. He was loth to admit he had bedded a wench Francis himself had first recommended to him. 'I did, but now she is wed to a squire.'

'No matter,' said Francis charitably. 'She will serve me well tonight, for as I remember she is a gallant mount. She was a fine nag to ride once, as I and several of my courtiers found. Then I deprive you of naught you treasure, brother?'

'Have her, and welcome,' Henry said harshly, then remembering his aim to outdo Francis in kingly splendour, added, 'But I could find you a worthier mate if you wish it.'

'No, no, my English mare will suffice,' Francis drawled, and draining his goblet, he embraced Henry and bade him goodnight. In a furious mood of frustration Henry stamped back to the royal pavilion where Catherine lay already snoring, deeply asleep.

It was a startled Mary who found, not the King of England but the King of France stealing softly into her tent that night, but with all the warmth of her passionate, responsive nature which could say nay to no man, she opened her arms to him willingly. It was only later, as he lay stroking her long hair and murmuring phrases calculated to rouse her yet again, that she remembered Anne's revelation that she was in love with Francis, and Mary pitied her. From the love-lorn look in Anne's large dark eyes it was evident she would willingly change places with her sister at this moment.

The day came when at last the two kings challenged each other to a wrestling bout, and to Mary's dismay Francis threw Henry to the ground. Henry rose, his pink face puzzled and disbelieving, then changed to a scowl of resentment. Queen Catherine and Queen Claude were at great pains to avert a quarrel, but Francis' handsome protestations that he had merely caught Henry off-balance and thus thrown him unfairly, saved the delicate situation. Henry, with great effort, managed to wipe the scowl from his face and contrive a thin smile, but tonight, he vowed inwardly, Francis would not rob him of Mary's comfort again. And it was a somewhat pathetic figure, limping slightly from his bruises, who eagerly welcomed Mary to his tent when the valet fetched her thither.

Mary was so overjoyed to feel his great arms enfold her once again that she neither noticed his discomfort nor gave a thought to where Carey might be. Henry had seen to it that his gentleman was engaged elsewhere, and now his small bright eyes roved possessively over Mary's form, coming to rest on the pert plump breasts and full buttocks. Her eyes were wide and eager, her lips parted, and he could hear her soft, quick breaths of desire. Wrenching at the buttons of his velvet doublet as though they were of some base metal and not finest gold, he cast the doublet aside and grasped her tightly, muttering hoarsely the while,

'Mary of the moonlight, how I have missed you, child! Come, embrace me, enfold me as only you know how.'

'I too have languished for you, Sire,' she began to whisper as her gown slid to the carpeted floor, but Henry stopped her mouth firmly. Deprived for so long, there was no delay, no delicacy in Henry now. He had had enough these many days of Gallic courtesy and politesse, and now it was time for good, straightforward English action.

If Mary found him on this occasion a trifle coarser and hastier than before, she made no complaint. On the contrary, her heart was full of joy that after so long she and her masterful Henry were reunited over more. She clung eagerly, returning ardent kiss for kiss, passionate caress for caress, feeling herself melt into frantic desire for him. And when, by the moonlight he swore suited her so well, he escorted her back to her own tent, she found nothing odd in the fact that in the space of three nights three entirely different men had slumbered over her soft-limbed body.

CHAPTER SEVENTEEN

PAS SEUL

TORRENTIAL midsummer rain lashed the Val Doré into a quagmire before the great festivity ended, but no leaden sky could depress Mary's spirits. Henry had come back to her, and it was evident that one of her family at least did not scorn and reject her, and for that she was grateful to Anne. They parted with many tears and kisses, and once more Mary glimpsed the lovelight in Anne's eyes when she looked upon Francis, a molten gaze of pain and pleasure.

Once again in England it seemed as though His Grace no longer considered it necessary to conceal his activities so carefully. If he took Mary to ride with him in the royal barge or to watch him hunt and joust, Will Carey seemed discreetly not to notice. Nor did the Queen comment.

Thomas Boleyn still spoke little to his daughter, though the favours which came his way began to soften his attitude a little. When all the Court knows a man has been appointed Controller of the Household, junior only to the Treasurer and the Lord Steward, on account of his daughter's willing ways with the King, one cannot remain completely aloof. And when further titles begin to accrue — Master of the Hunt, Chamberlain of Tonbridge, Keeper of the Manor of Penshurst — one can afford to unbend and smile fractionally once in a while. So if the King required a little seclusion with his mistress occasionally, Hever Castle was at his disposal. And if Lady Beth lumbered slowly to a conclusion that the strictest propriety was not being observed in her domain, she was wise enough to hold her tongue.

Mary herself was extremely content. Throughout the winter Henry was attentive and as ardent as she could wish, but in the spring clouds threatened the hitherto peaceful horizon between England and France, and Sir Thomas feared for his younger daughter's safety.

'Fret not, Thomas, we shall recall our subjects from France immediately,' Henry assured him. Soon word came that Anne and the Lady Jane Seymour amongst others had embarked for home.

'I would I could go down to Hever to welcome Anne.' Mary confided to Will. Her husband put his arm comfortingly around her shoulders.

'You have but to ask and doubtless the Queen will give you leave,' he said, and Mary noted once again his tactful omission of the King's name. He could have said His Grace would grant aught his cherished mistress wished, but kindly forbearance forbade such indiscretion.

Consent to Mary's absence from Court was granted without question, and she found herself once more in her father's moated manor house at the chillest time of year. Lady Beth's rosy face lighted with happiness at seeing her, no vestige of reproach marring her country-fresh face though she undoubtedly knew well of Mary's position now, with the King.

'It is good to see you child,' she said, simply, holding Mary to her ample bosom, 'and presently we shall have Anne home too. Soon we shall be a family again, for I have missed you all sorely.'

Hever's atmosphere wrapped itself warmly about Mary, the scent of pine-logs on the fires and fresh-strewn rushes and the peace that pervaded the place in Father's absence giving her a blissful feeling of contentment. At last the date came when Anne was expected, and Lady Beth was near distracted with joyful anticipation.

Mary stared at the leafless trees lining the drive, seeing not them but her lively, laughing sister.

And suddenly she was here, but Mary could only stand and stare at the haughty woman tersely ordering the disposal of her baggage, tossing her gloves to a maid, and bidding Lady Beth good day as though she had seen her only yesterday. It was Anne indeed, the slight figure and slanting black eyes confirmed it, but it was as though a stranger stood in the vestibule. A cool kiss on Mary's cheek, and then she turned, smiling, to her stepmother who hovered uncomfortably, uncertain whether to clasp this elegant lady familiarly or not.

'T'is good to see you well, Mother,' Anne said brightly, 'and you too sister. I am freezing – and famished. Is there food ready, Mother?'

A wide-eyed Lady Beth and Mary sat at table with the exotic creature who picked daintily at her food, her bright eyes darting from one entranced face to the other as she ate and talked. Neither could believe that this gorgeously-clad figure in velvet and lynx fur was truly Anne, so different she seemed. Still the same vital, graceful woman, but there was something slightly unnatural about her quick, high laugh with a note of near-hysteria in it, and the voluble chatter loaded with witty aphorisms which went above their heads. The old Anne had been bright and attractive, but this one, with her Frenchified ways, was sparklingly brilliant and cold. Like a diamond, Mary thought wistfully, fascinating and beautiful but hard and unfeeling. Something had wrought a change in Anne, and she sensed it was some event which had brought great sorrow in its train.

In Anne's bedchamber that night, with half-emptied boxes spewing a trail of fine lace gowns and basques, of mantles and slippers about the room, Mary sat on the bed and pondered how to break into her sister's constant talk to discover the reason for the change.

'Do you like my collar?' Anne demanded, bending gracefully to lift one from a coffer. 'It is a fashion I introduced at the French Court. Now everyone wears them. I
must endeavour to influence our English Court too, if I
can be introduced there, for I see by your gown that
English ladies are not so fashionable yet.'

'I am not so wealthy as most,' Mary remarked, not out
of envy but because it was true.

'Nor I, but my admirers in France kept me well supp-
lied with trinkets and stuffs. From what I hear you
too should be liberally endowed with gowns and the like.'

Mary fingered the fine cambric of a nightgown without
comment, yet wondering whether her sister had indeed
taken lovers in France. She was not beautiful, it was
true, but she had such a fascinating way about her, the
way she walked and tossed her small head, that men must
find her very appealing. She stared at Anne. There was a
coldness about her, and a tightness to the otherwise
sensual lips. It must have been a lover who had mal-
treated her, Mary decided in a flash of intuition. Anne
would not give herself lightly, and if she did she would
expect the same unreserved love in return. Mary rose and
went across to her sister, putting her hands on her should-
ders.

'Tell me, Nan. Let us talk as we used to, here in this
bed in the old days. Remember? Tell me what happened
in France. Did you have many lovers?'

Anne's sharp bright eyes focussed on Mary in scorn.
'I did not! I am no wanton, though I do not judge others
for what they do.'

'Then a lover, one special lover?' Mary persisted quietly. To her surprise she felt the thin shoulders under her
fingers begin to tremble, and saw the quick tears that
sprang to Anne's eyes.

'What makes you think that, may I ask?' Anne retorted
sharply, brushing away Mary's hands and turning to look

in the silver mirror. 'You can see I am no beauty. Look at me, thin and flat, far from fair and curving as you are.' Her voice was edged with bitterness as she spoke. She tore at the jewelled collar about her throat. 'And see, I am blemished with what fools believe is the devil's mark, here on my throat, and this —' She thrust out her hand, revealing the tiny stump of a rudimentary sixth finger on her hand. 'What man, think you, would choose a maid with all these faults?'

Although her back was turned to Mary, her sister could detect the tremble that shook her frame and the hysterical note in her voice which belied her words. Mary came closer, placing her hands again on Anne's shoulders.

'Once before in this room you spoke those words, Nan, saying how ill-featured you were and how the village children feared you. I told you then you were no less comely than I, for we are very alike. But I fear it hurts you still that people believe you a witch, does it not?'

Anne's hands covered her face in an attempt to conceal the tears, but from beneath her fingers Mary could hear the sobbing voice.

'God grant that I had been a witch, Mall, and he would not have escaped thus lightly.'

Mary drew her, unresistingly, to sit on the bed. 'Tell me, Nan. Who was he?'

After a moment Anne drew herself upright, blinking back the tears and speaking in a more composed voice. 'I had not meant to tell you aught, nor anyone else, of what has passed. I tell you now, Mall, only on your solemn vow never to speak of this again, neither to me nor to anyone. I wish to forget it ever happened.'

'I swear,' said Mary.

Anne's dark eyes gazed into the distance, as if groping back in time and space. 'It was soon after we met at Ardres, remember? I think I let slip to you then I was smitten with King Francis.' She paused a moment and gulped, as though the effort of speaking his name was too great for her. Mary tactfully remained silent.

'Damn his soul.' Anne's voice was bitter with hatred. Mary gasped. 'The cold, callous swine,' Anne went on, her voice rising again. 'For months he must have known how I adored him, yet he took one Court wench after another and only played at coquetry with me.'

Mary's round eyes widened. 'But — you hate him?'

Anne flashed black, hate-filled eyes at her. 'As you would too, perhaps, were you not so eager to bed with any lusty man. I sought none for my bed — only Francis, and he knew it. In the end, he sought me, or so I believed. He wooed me so persuasively, so gently, that though I longed to leap into his arms I held back until he was mad with passion for me. He vowed undying love. He swore he would not cast me off as he did others.'

'And — and you believed him?'

'The more fool I. Only an idiot crazed with love as I was would do so, I know it now, but I was but a green thing.'

Anne rose slowly and crossed to look out of the window at the rimefrosted fields below Hever. 'I loved him, Mall, I adored him, and though every courtier in France was on his knees for me, I gave myself only to Francis. I, who swore never to love any man more than I was loved, gave my girlish heart to an unfeeling wretch who sought only to use women and then abandon them.'

A sob choked her. Mary came to put her arms about her sister, understanding fully now. Had not she too been seduced by the same fair words from Francis, but thankfully had escaped with her heart intact since she had not hoped for so much as Anne? Her murmured words of comfort were abruptly interrupted.

'No, do not speak of it! I have no time for pity nor comfort, Mall, for it is over.' The black eyes glittered again in the moonlight. 'But I wished then I were a witch

Mall, for I would have given him a love potion, or failing that, laid a curse upon him that would have shrivelled his lying body to a putrescent, mouldering heap!'

Mary shrank in horror. 'Oh Nan! Say not such evil things! It is not you to speak so viciously!'

Anne laughed sardonically. 'It was not me, sister, but you will discover how I have changed. Henceforth I shall love no man, I swear it, but he that is foolish enough to love me shall pay for it dearly.'

'Nan! You would punish others for Francis' sins!'

Anne spun round angrily. 'And why not, pray? Are not all men tarred with the same evil thoughts, designing, predatory creatures? Think you your Henry is any different from the rest? He too will cast you off like a tattered glove when another wench catches his lecherous eye! He uses you only because you are fair and soft and willing and ask naught, like a great, mindless feather bed! Name me a man who is not self-centred, if you can!'

'My husband,' Mary ventured softly. Anne gaped at her for a moment, her dark eyes still and startled for once, then she laughed shrilly.

'Your husband? Will Carey, the blind, dumb, deaf Court jester? All the world knows it is a convenient marriage indeed, Mary Carey, where the husband is too weak and stupid to save his wife from the King's clutches. You call Will Carey a man? Pah, you make me sick. He is as self-centred as the rest, for in his silence lies his advantage.'

Mary felt the quick prick of tears behind her eyelids at hearing Will thus maligned, but she held silent. Anne's vicious words, she felt, sprang from her own hurt and not from a wish to hurt Mary.

'Will loves me,' she said softly, 'and that gives me cause for contentment.'

'And the King?' Anne jeered.

'He loves me too, I know it. As I love him.'

'But the day will come when he cares no longer for you,

and what will you have gained from it, may I ask? No title, no mansion even. You are a fool, Mary Carey.'

'I shall be happy, knowing I have been loved.'

'Used rather, and scorned, as Father and George despise you.'

Mary's gaze fell sorrowfully. 'It saddens me that Father finds me disappointing, of course, but Lady Beth does not.'

Anne's expression softened. 'Indeed, our stepmother is a dear, sweet creature and there is not an ounce of dissimultation in her plump, lovable body. I shall be glad of Lady Beth's cheerful company.'

'Then perhaps you will tell her of Francis?'

Anne's reply was swift and decisively direct. 'No, never! I love her, but I cannot confide in her. Oh, Mall, such dark and devious torments there are in my soul that even I cannot understand the turbulence at times, let alone a simple creature like Lady Beth. I tell you this, Mary, henceforth I shall love and trust no one — you hear me? No one. From this day on I shall seek only what is good for me.'

She turned away to reach for her nightgown, and Mary understood the gesture of dismissal. As she walked quietly from the chamber sorrow weighed heavily on her, for the change that had come about in her sister was undoubtedly an evil one which could lead only to evil consequences one day.

CHAPTER EIGHTEEN

VIBRATO

TROUBLED though Mary was about her sister's bitterness she kept her word and did not refer to it again. In time, she hoped, perhaps Anne would fall in love again and the mellowing influence would soften her icy heart. With a sigh, Mary returned to Court.

Henry, his arms empty over-long in Mary's absence, welcomed her back enthusiastically, enquiring belatedly how, her sister fared. Within a few months he informed Mary that the old Duke of Norfolk, enchanted with his niece's polished Gallic manners and elegance, was requesting a place at Court for her.

'So your sister too is to come to Placentia to serve the Queen,' Henry said. 'There, does not that please you my love?'

And indeed it was pleasing to Mary, to have Anne sharing chambers close by her own and to see how popular her sister rapidly became at Court. Brother George exhibited Anne proudly, her lively manner and quick wit, her gay laughter and teasing coquetry quickly earning her a following of admirers, amongst them her own cousin, Tom Wyatt. Mary smiled contentedly. If ever Anne had cause to doubt her own attraction and decry her lack of beauty, this constant following of clever, gifted young men who like Tom, wrote poems in her praise, must surely undo the harm.

Nor was Will slow to notice the attention Anne drew upon herself. In fact it was he who first pointed out to Mary how her sister seemed to have ensnared even serious young Henry Percy, heir to the Duke of Northumberland

and now a gentleman of Wolsey's household at York Palace. With his master he came often to the Court.

'And always his eyes linger on your sister with that earnest, soulful look which can only betoken love,' Will commented.

'He and many others, it seems,' Mary replied. 'I always said Anne was far more fetching than she realised. Soon she may have her pick of any man at Court if she thinks to take herself a husband.'

But in the matter of a husband for Anne Sir Thomas had already forestalled her. Most evenings Anne came late to Mary's chamber to recount her day's doings, how she watched a bear-baiting in the inner palace courtyard or played the lute while the gentlemen listened enraptured. Always her black eyes glowed with pleasure as she spoke of her activities, and particularly the night she had taken part with His Grace himself in a masked revel, and allegory of love called the *Château Vert*. Though Henry had not noticed her among the many silver-clad ladies who graced the revel, he being too engrossed with his own part as the Knight of Ardent Desire, it had nevertheless given her enormous pleasure.

But one night Anne's entry into Mary's chamber was a furious crashing flounce which betrayed that something was amiss. Dismissing her maid, Mary sat attentively and waited.

'It is too much! Father over-reaches himself!' Anne blurted out when at last the door closed. 'Do you know what he plans to do, just as I am enjoying life at Court so well? He thinks to marry me off to some Irish lack-wit and bundle me off to live with him in the Irish bogs! I'll have none of it!'

'Pray, come sit by me and tell me clearly,' Mary said soothingly. 'What Irish lack-wit, and why?'

'James Butler, son of Sir Piers Butler, with whom our father has wrangled these many years over our estates in

Ireland. Both have laid claim so long to the Ormond lands, that now Father, abetted by our uncle Surrey, sees fit to marry a Boleyn to a Butler and hence seal a bargain. But I'll not be traded like some prize heifer for a parcel of land, that I'll not!'

Anne clenched her hands, stuffing her knuckles into her mouth to stem the tears of rage. Mary took her hands, stroking them to allay her anger.

'It is our duty, Nan, to obey Father.'

Anne fumed. 'It is all very well for you, Mall, since you are wed already! Even for George, Father chose a wife whom George hates! Now I am the only one who remains that he can use for his bartering, but I swear I shall not be used again. No, never as long as I live!'

'But what can you do?'

Anne's lashes fluttered downward. 'I cannot marry James Butler in any event, for there is another. I have told Father I love another man, and he me.'

Blue eyes widened. 'You love? Oh Anne, I am so pleased for you. But who is he?'

'Henry Percy.'

Mary gasped. Of all the gay, lively young men who surrounded Anne with adulation, it was incredible that she had chosen one so timid and gauche, one brought up in the solitude of Wressel Castle far from the courtly life.

'And — what did Father say?' she ventured.

'He is to leave at dawn on the King's business, and by the time he returns in a week I am to have come to my senses. He says the King had already agreed to my marriage with Butler.' Anne's voice was cool and matter-of-fact now.

'What shall you do, Anne?'

'Refuse, of course, I shall have Henry Percy or no one.'

'Oh, Nan, do you dare to defy Father — and His Grace?'

Anne faced her coolly. 'I do, and I shall. As I promised you, Mall, I shall choose what is best for me, and Father

and your beloved Henry too can go hang for aught I care.
My mind is resolute, Mall. I shall have none of James
Butler.'

'He is a pleasant enough fellow Anne, not the graceless
peasant you might think. He has spent much time here at the
Court — I have seen him myself — and is a passably agreeable fellow.'

'Passably agreeable!' Anne snorted. 'What care I for
your passably agreeable fellows? I will not have him,
and that is resolved.'

Her mouth was resolutely set and her head stubbornly
high as she left Mary, and her sister could only hope
that a week's grace would soften Anne's mulishness, for
naught but trouble could result else. It would be a pity
for Anne to marry one man when she loved another, but
others had done it before her.

Throughout the week Mary's gaze was drawn to Anne
and the doting Percy who somehow found it his business
to visit Court frequently without his master Wolsey.
Mary noted how Anne lowered her lashes demurely when
she spoke with him, tossing her head gaily in laughter
at some little joke, and mincing and swaying as she
passed him when they danced the Hey. And on one occasion
Mary even saw them emerging from a shady arbour next to
one of the yew-walks, their eyes shining and a faint
blush tinging Anne's pale cheek.

Sir Thomas's reappearance at Court was typically brusque
and direct. He found Mary and Anne alone together, embroidering in a solar.

'Well, madam?' he demanded. Neither Anne nor Mary
spoke. 'Well, Mistress Anne, I demand to know your decision,' he repeated. 'Will you marry James Butler or no?'

Anne kept her dark eyes bent to her work. 'I will not,
Father. As I told you, I love another.'

Sir Thomas came a menacing step closer. 'Do you mean,
Percy, child? Then know he is not free to marry you. He

is already betrothed to the Lady Mary Talbot, daughter of the Earl of Shrewsbury.'

Mary saw the triumphant glitter in his eyes that revealed he believed he had Anne beaten. His younger daughter looked up from her work and stared back at him with the same determined gleam.

'That I know, for he told me. But still he wishes to marry me, and I him. I will have none of your James Butler, Father.'

She rose gracefully, putting her work to one side, and walked sedately from the room. Sir Thomas's face darkened with rage and, cursing under his breath, he strode out after her.

Mary was dumbfounded at Anne's daring, and fearful for the consequences. She knew her Father was a vengeful soul when he was crossed, and he would never submit to defeat at the hands of his own youngest child. The punishment was sure to be terrifying when Sir Thomas crossed swords with a spirit as stubborn and wilful as his own.

Retribution was swift. Wolsey summoned the Earl of Northumberland to come south to deal with his recalcitrant son, and the enraged father lost no time in publicly berating Percy before dragging him home to Wressel Castle, to honour his troth to the Lady Mary.

Sullen rage burned in Anne's eyes as she came to bid farewell to Mary. 'I too have been sent from Court in disgrace,' she muttered savagely. 'Back home to Hever, to moulder and rot far from all the life and gaiety here. Oh, Mall, I shall wither and die in the dismal countryside! Come and visit me soon, will you not?'

Mary assured her that she would. 'I shall be thinking of you constantly,' Anne added, pausing in the doorway to draw her scarlet cloak about her. 'And of those I hate.'

'Hate? Oh, Anne!' Mary exclaimed reproachfully.

'Wolsey above all, for foiling my plan. And Father for

his ruthlessness.'

'You should think only of love and kindliness, Anne — treasure the love you bore for Henry Percy.' Mary's gaze was tender as she recalled the sight of the delicate, spindly-legged youth as he rode sorrowfully out of Greenwich for the last time, miserably following his irate father homeward. 'Poor Harry! I fear he will take this matter worse than you, Anne, for you are stronger than he.'

'Harry Percy?' Anne's voice was light with amusement. 'He is another I hate, Mall, for his feeble weakness, the gutless sheep.'

Shock caused Mary to gasp audibly. 'Hate him? But you loved him, Anne, you said so! You refused Butler because you wanted to marry Percy!'

'Said I so? Dear heaven, I must learn to be more accurate, must I not? I admit it was a little mendacious Mall, but I had to contrive to avoid the Butler creature somehow. No, my dear sister, I did not want to marry Harry Percy only to use him to my advantage. Did I not tell you once that henceforth men should be for my use, and not I for theirs? Fret not for me, Mary, for I shall find the way yet to what I wish to achieve.'

'And — what do you want, Anne?'

Scarlet shoulders shrugged, and a mischievous gleam leapt into Anne's dark eyes. 'I know not yet, but it shall be something more than a Northumbrian duke who is too gawky to know how to kiss a maid, and more than an Irish pig-peasant, whatever his lands and title. At Hever I shall have time to ponder and plan. Farewell, Mall, and pray come visit me soon.'

With a quick hug and kiss she was gone. Wonderingly, Mary began to lave and perfume herself, donning the heavy citron taffeta gown that Henry favoured, for to-night he was to visit her again. And he would be eager and ardent, she knew, for he had been much occupied of late, entertaining the Emperor Charles yet again on a prolonged visit. It was probable he had not yet heard of Anne and Percy's disgrace, for Wolsey was quite able to deal with that matter without reference to his royal master.

At the right moment of repose after passion, Mary broached the subject of Anne's dismissal to Henry. He yawned sleepily and drew her closer.

'I did hear tell of the incident, Mall, but it seems that your sister was treated fairly. After all, her disobedience to Sir Thomas after he had secured my royal agreement to her wedding with James Butler too, is not a trivial offence. Nor is Percy's slighting of his betrothal vows to another. No, it seems best that your sister retires to the country for a time and there, perchance, the wayward wench will think on her behaviour and learn a little submissiveness. Were she pliant like you, my sweeting, no one could deny her aught.'

With a disarming smile he took Mary in his arms again, the subject of the errant Anne already dismissed from his mind, but Mary was determined not to relinquish the subject so easily.

'You know my sister, Sire, since you know her to be wayward?' she ventured between kisses.

'I have seen her about the Court, but know her little. She is too black and lean for my liking, and has an icy air about her. A creature of winter and midnight, while you, my jewel, are of springtime and lushness. Come, let me stroke your buttercup hair and gaze into bluebell eyes the while. Let us prate no more of your swarthy sister.'

This time the note of finality in Henry's voice precluded the mention of Anne's name again, and Mary forgot all else in the contentment of savouring Henry's love. And in the months that followed Henry, though indulging Mary in every possible way else, remained obdurately deaf to the subject of Anne.

It was a long time before Mary found occasion to visit her sister, but to her surprise she found Anne apparently contented enough with life at Hever. Surrounded by fresh-plucked rose-blooms which she was arranging, Anne's dark beauty was becomingly set off.

'Lady Beth and I suit each other well and enjoy Hever while Father is absent,' Anne remarked. 'Only now and then I grow wistful and long for the company of George and the others. But I will be patient, for I am certain Father will arrange my recall in time.'

But the months slipped into years and no recall came. Mary, flattered by Henry's constant devotion, forgot to fret over Anne, and in the moments she did recollect with a twinge of regret, she remembered Lady Beth's words at their last encounter.

'Fret not for Anne, Mary, for she knows what she wants of this world, and sooner or later she will see to it that she obtains it. I have never known such a determined maid. She bides her time only to improve on it later.'

Her words recalled Mary's own mother's words as she lay dying. Anne and George will carve their own destiny, Mother had said, and since Lady Beth who, despite her apparent simplicity was a good judge of character, deemed likewise, then who was Mary to argue? She herself had risen far above Mother's dreams, adored mistress of the King, and to her certain knowledge, his only mistress. Unlike most Kings in Europe, Henry was remarkably faithful, and Mary was extremely content.

Will Carey too still remained devotedly at heel, solicitous and silent as always. Like some faithful spaniel he hovered solemn-eyed always near and within call, disappearing unobtrusively when the great vibrant figure of his King approached. Mary basked in the warmth of Henry's amorous approval, and if the Queen noted how beautifully apparelled and adorned her lady appeared, she looked away. Henry, for his part, did not flaunt Mary at Court, yet she was respected as only the mistress of a King could be.

Sir Thomas's attitude towards his elder daughter became noticeably warmer, for during the long period of Anne's absence from Court and Mary's splendid favour with the King his career blossomed.

'Knight of the Garter!' he crowed enthusiastically to Mary, joy for once lighting his saturnine face in place of the eternal scowl. Stewardships rolled his way and then, to crown his joy, he was created a peer.

'Viscount of Rochford! Does not the title suit me well?' he preened. 'And George is to be granted a manor of his own in Norfolk! Continue to conduct yourself agreeably Mary, and who knows what else may not follow?'

Now, he was convinced, the Boleyns' fortunes would surely soar yet higher with the fairest daughter in her heyday in the monarch's esteem. For five years now Mary had ruled Henry's potentially fickle heart, and there was not the faintest flicker of a change in his attitude. For Mary herself life was joyful, darkened only by momentary regret when she occasionally saw Anne.

'Two years and more I have spent alone here with step-mother,' Anne said, a hint of irritation in her voice further betrayed by the testy manner in which hre slim fingers plucked the petals one by one from a marigold. 'It is too long for my brain to lie idle, tested by nothing more exacting then potting preserves and stitching a sampler. Mary, I want to come back to London with you. Nay more, I *need* to return to where there is life and conversation and gaiety, or I swear I shall die of boredom else. Hever is so dull, with naught but an occasional visit from George or Tom Wyatt — and you too, of course — to enliven my day. They bring me the vitality and exuberance I crave, Mall, and the more they tease me with witty jests and riddles the more I yearn to be back at Court, to coquette and be gay, and be surrounded constantly by such people.'

She paused, looking up from the mangled flower to gaze

deep into Mary's troubled eyes, her own large and darkly eloquent.

'Please, Mall, I beg you, speak with the King for me, or I fear I shall pine away alone here.'

'I have tried, Nan, I have truly, but though he grants me all else, he is deaf to this one request.' Blue eyes brimmed with tears as they looked into black, pleading eyes. Then pleading changed to eagerness.

'Then bring his Grace down here to Hever, and give me the chance to plead with him myself. Oh, Mall, he will not refuse me when he sees how I fret and pine. I only want to return to Greenwich. He is reckoned to be a generous man — he cannot deny me that!'

Mary took her sister's thin fingers in her own plump, beringed hands. 'Sweetheart, if he sees you as I do now I think he cannot. It is some time since we visited Hever together, Henry and I, so presently I shall suggest it to him.

'Have patience, Nan. I will bring Henry here and leave you the opportunity to plead with him. No man could refuse such beautiful black eyes, I know it. Gladly I shall bring him to you.'

CHAPTER NINETEEN

DIMINUENDO

LADY Beth was extremely agitated when she welcomed His Grace and Mary to Hever, bobbing and curtseying nervously as she babbled apology.

'Your Grace, I crave your pardon that Mistress Anne is not here to greet you with me. I sought her high and low but she is nowhere to be found, the mischievous maid. Forgive her, Your Grace. Her youth, you know.'

After a goblet of wine Henry left Mary with Lady Beth to stroll in the lengthening shadows of evening in the park. It was a bright-eyed Anne who returned by his side, hands folded in seeming meekness but eager light in her almond eyes.

'It is done!' she confided eagerly to Mary.

'So soon? But how?'

'It was not difficult. To find a maid alone beneath a tree, strumming a lute and singing a song of one's own composition is flattering to any man, and King Henry is but a man, after all.'

'His own song? But how came you to know of it?'

'From George, of course, who helped him compose the lyric, how else? His Grace was enchanted by my singing and complimented me on my voice and playing. Then he commented how tall and graceful I had grown, far more comely than he remembered me. From there, Mall, it was but a step to convince him his court had need of ladies such as I.'

'Then you are to return with us to Greenwich?' Mary said in surprise, though pleasure rippled for her sister's fortune.

'Not yet, but soon, Mall. His Grace will let it be known to Father that he considers I have now expiated my sin and may return.' Anne could not resist a little skip of joy before composing herself to enter the great hall demurely, where King Henry and Lady Beth already sat at table while the stewards scurried about them. Mary saw Anne's eyelashes drop coyly as her glance encountered Henry's, before seating herself gracefully at his side.

As she had predicted, not many months passed before Anne reappeared at Placentia, bringing with her a whole new atmosphere to the Court. Life and verve seemed to throb about her, the younger courtiers clustering about her, female eyes glinting with envy while male eyes gleamed in approbation. Coquetry, the favourite Court pastime, suited Anne well. She knew intuitively how to tease and lure, to hold out unspoken promise with veiled eyes without ever committing herself. Mary watched contentedly. Anne was undoubtedly happy now, secure in such open attention.

It was cousin Tom Wyatt whose admiration first altered into love for the pert, flashing-eyed maid of honour. Tied to a loveless marriage, he nevertheless made no effort to conceal his adoration for Anne, declaring his love in his constant sonnets and epigrams.

'What word is that that changeth not
Though it be turned and made in twain?
It is mine answer, God it wot,
And eke the causer of my pain.'

Anne read the parchment out aloud before an assembled crowd of courtiers, smiling the while.

'A riddle, Tom, for me?' she dimpled. Murmurs could be heard among the crowd. 'Anna, Anna is the answer, spelt the same back and forth.' Mary glanced at Henry's eager, interested face. He had guessed the answer to the riddle, and a new emotion was being born, Mary could read it in his face. It was a challenge, and Henry could never resist a challenge. If his lively, clever young courtiers whose company he craved in order to cling to his own youth were playing this game of pursuing Anne Boleyn, this game of chivalry with its courtly code of etiquette, then he too must accept the challenge. It was an exciting game, the pursuit of an elusive, quicksilver woman who would prove a difficult quarry. Mary read the meaning in Henry's gaze and felt a quiver of doubt ripple in her breast.

The following evening Henry had begun the chase, reading aloud a lyric of his own to which he had composed music, and then he asked Anne to sing it for him. Mary's blue eyes watched his proud expression as he listened, his auburn hair beginning to thin just a little, and his chin thrust into a jewelled hand. In his green velvet doublet slashed with silver, and his collar of magnificent gems, he looked a fine figure, and Mary's heart melted at his eager boyishness as he smiled at Anne. Her clear low voice sang the words he himself had written of her, of catching the breeze in a net, and though her name was not mentioned, it was clear she knew the King himself had joined the chase.

It was but a game, a pastime every clever young man pursued, Mary reassured herself. It had no meaning beyond that. It would be foolish not to expect Henry to exercise his considerable skills in versifying and lyric-writing as George and Tom and all the fashionable, admired young men did. Henry was but thirty-four and extremely handsome and talented. He would not wish to be regarded as any less a man than the others.

By day Henry hunted still and wrestled and jousted and by night he came faithfully to Mary's bed, passionate and ardent as ever. But by evening amid his courtiers as he played confidently on the flute or the virginals, his small blue eyes rested on the slender figure of Anne. Eventually

Mary could no longer resist mentioning it to Anne.

'So he does,' Anne agreed coolly, 'and Tom and many others besides, but what of that? It is but a game.'

More lyrics to Anne poured from Henry's quill.

'Now unto my lady promise to her I make
From all other only to her I me betake.'

His Grace was being charitable, Mary decided, paying attention to Anne to atone for her long banishment and neglect, or perhaps to pay tribute to the Boleyn family, who always cared for his needs so loyally.

But when Anne, still following the rules of conduct of this game of chivalry, began bestowing tokens on her admirers, giving a jewelled tablet to Tom Wyatt and then a ring to Henry, matters became more involved. Henry enjoyed a challenge well enough, Mary knew, but he also enjoyed being the winner in a contest. Defeat was loathsome to him, as she remembered from the day when King Francis threw him at wrestling. And if Anne gave tokens to others besides himself, he was not winning. His face reddened and his little eyes grew narrower when he looked on Tom Wyatt, and Mary recognised the sign of jealousy.

Her sister saw it too, and to Mary's dismay she deliberately began to play off one suitor against the other. Mary caught her breath in trepidation. Her sister did not know Henry as she did, or she would realise it was unwise to invoke his anger so. She decided to speak warningly to Anne.

Anne shrugged. 'It is of no account now. I told His Grace Tom took the tablet from me, that I did not give it to him willingly. His Grace is easily placated, for he believed me and sent me away smiling.'

'You lied to Henry?'

'Why not? I will not be sent from Court again, and so long as I vex him not, I am safe.'

'He — admires you, Anne, and is jealous of Tom.'

'I know it. But Tom is to travel to Italy with his friend

Russell soon, so His Grace need not fret.'

Mary marvelled how Anne could treat the King so lightly, as though he were but a child to be humoured. It was a dangerous tactic to adopt with a creature as volatile and changeable as Henry could be. And just as this time Henry was appearing to be less decisive, more changeable than usual. Unexpected events seemed to keep cropping up which made him appear less frequently in Mary's chamber at night. Henry was apologetic and full of regret, but perhaps tomorrow . . .

Mary was never able to pinpoint the exact moment at which she detected Henry's drifting attention, when she sensed that his hitherto unstinted adoration of her was waning. It was a flicker of unease, swifting swept aside, that kept returning to nag her. It was a cruel, vindictive thought to believe that her sister was deliberately diverting Henry's attentions. No, of course not, it was this lighthearted game of coquetry only, nothing more.

There was more time now to see Will Carey of an evening, and it was he who was astute enough to detect what Mary had missed.

'Your sister is very like you, Mall, only dark where you are fair, but her temperament is very different. I have no doubt the King first noticed her because she reminds him of you, and after that her vitality attracted him the more.'

He was speaking only of the King's pursuit of Anne in this game of chivalry, for he would not willingly hurt Mary, but she could see beyond his words. He was right, this gentle, observant Carey: it was Anne's gaiety and cleverness which fascinated the King where Mary was reserved, simple and totally lacking in Anne's wit. A greyness settled over Mary. After all these years — how long now? For six years Henry had come faithfully to her and to no other mistress, and after so long it seemed inevitable that she was losing him.

But to her own sister, there was the irony of it. Mary

felt her heart contract with pain and sadness. Though she bore Anne no ill-will, she was saddened for both her and Henry.

Henry's eyes devoured Anne as the courtiers sat listening to his lute, his eager fingers plucking the strings. By now it was obvious to everyone, Mary realised with a stab of anguish, that he adored Anne, who capriciously flirted still and held him at bay.

Henry came to Mary's chamber. For the first time he did not carry her to the bed, but stood fidgeting by the chair. He wore the bemused expression of a child who has erred and knows not how to apologise or atone.

'Mary, I love your sister,' he blurted out at length. Strange how Henry, normally so suave and polished a courtier with a string of easy phases, seemed now so at a loss, Mary thought wryly. He was standing twisting the huge jewels on his fingers. In a moment he would find the words to tell her it was over, how sorry he was, how he appreciated her.

'Mall — oh Mall! You have always been so gentle, so understanding. Tell me now what I should do.' He sank into the chair, covering his face with his hands, the russet crown of his head glowing ruddy in the firelight.

'Do, Sire?'

'How to gain her, for she is like ice and I cannot reach her. When I think she is in my grasp she melts through my fingers like water. Oh, Mall! I must have her! I must! Tell me how!'

Waves of giddiness surged over Mary. She sank on to the bed and waited until the nausea had receded a little, before replying.

'Are you — in love with Anne?'

'I adore her! She is the most magical, bewitching creature I have ever set eyes on, and my heart is bleeding for desire of her! You know her best, Mall, so tell me, I beg you, how I may win her.'

And that was all. No word of apology or regret. No word of appreciation for six years of joyful love and fidelity. Just a selfish demand to have his own burning desire fulfilled. Mary sat silent, sickened, nauseated beyond words.

'Forgive me, Mall,' the King's voice muttered brokenly. 'I cannot help myself. I love your sister and by God's bones I swear I must have her.'

Then it had gone far beyond courtly convention, Mary realised bitterly. The game of flirtation, thrust and parry, witty remark and sparkling rejoinder had long been passed and left behind. Steadying herself with deliberation Mary rose from the bed and crossed to Henry, resting her hand on his bowed shoulder. He looked up, his normally ruddy face now pale and anguished.

'You make no reproach, Mall? You feel no bitterness towards me?'

'None, Sire. We cannot help our emotions.'

It came to her with a curious twisting in her breast that she had truly loved Henry all these years, that it was no mere gratification of the senses as it had been with Francis. She loved him still, and was hurt with him that he could not attain what he desired so passionately. Like a mother, she wanted to give her child what he wept for.

Anne would not listen. 'You are a fine sister, Mary, to attempt to procure me for your lover.'

'You are driving him mad with passion for you, Nan,' Mary pointed out quietly. 'He is capable of wreaking terrible harm if he is crossed. You do not know him as I do.'

'So we must pander to the spoilt child? Not I, by the faith! Do you as you have always done, Mary, and bend your will to others; but do not expect the same of me.'

Sorrowfully Mary watched the last of Henry's love for her wither and die as that for Anne blossomed. Sadly she watched his wistful face and frenzied tempers when pursuit of Anne remained fruitless. Frenetically he tried to please

Anne, heaping gifts and favours upon her, elevating her
brother George to be his cup-bearer, but Anne remained
chilly and aloof.

'I want no part of him,' she told Mary coldly. 'His
lecherous little eyes and predatory fat fingers sicken
me. I want only what he can obtain for me — riches,
titles, mansions if he will — but never his great cumber-
some body.'

Mary listened tearfully, the queasy feeling in her stomach surging again. Continually in these days of uneasy
atmosphere she felt sickly fingers clawing in her guts.

'What is to become of us all?' she sobbed softly. It
was evident Henry cared no more for her soft, welcoming
arms and the bereft, empty sensation was becoming more
and more unbearable. Will Carey stood close, reassuring
and warm.

'It is not wise for you to remain here at Court, Mary,' he
advised her. 'Let me take you down to the country, away
to peace where you will not fret.'

Mary, dazed and bewildered, nodded agreement. To be
far away would be better than to stay and watch Anne's
cold disdain and Henry's tortured expression, knowing
he would never again come to her for comfort.

'Thank you, Will. I am sick at heart and weary of the
Court. I shall be glad to breathe the clean, fresh air
of Kent again and rid me of this foul hothouse atmosphere.'

Queen Catherine was kindly and even a shade regretful
at Mary's leave-taking, and Mary could not help but wonder
whether perhaps Her Grace feared her husband's exchange
of one amiable, undemanding mistress for another devious,
and more calculating one.

The cool, clear air of Hever breathed a soft benison on
Mary, gradually smoothing away the pain and bitterness.
And slowly the nausea whenever she thought of Henry's
powerful, masterful arms aching to enclose a thin, dark

figure, began to recede.

Will came down to visit her, and to her surprise he brought Anne with him, her tall, graceful figure cloaked in a magnificent new ermine-trimmed mantle. Undoubtedly Henry's gift, thought Mary, and momentarily the pain returned.

'What news, Anne?' she asked when they had embraced.

'None, save that I have decided to encourage your Henry after all. He will not gain the prize he seeks, not until I gain in return what I seek from him.'

'You speak in riddles, Anne. Please explain.'

Anne smiled. 'The Queen and he no longer live as man and wife, as you know. Now he would dispose of her to make way for me, so much he craves me. So I put it to him — circuitously, of course — that he divorces Her Grace. He thinks on it now. In time he will, and then I shall take her place.'

'In his bed, you mean?' Mary queried.

'You innocent! Have I not explained to you? He will marry me and make me Queen, or I shall never bed with him. Since he knows it, he will make me Queen. There now! Will not Father be pleased with me then?'

She twirled about the hall excitedly, like a child pleased with its own cleverness, while Mary clutched the back of a chair, her head spinning.

'Queen? You?' she gasped.

'Why not? We have noble blood already in our veins. It is not so unthinkable. Other Kings have divorced barren wives to take more fertile ones, so why not Henry?'

She stopped pacing and came back to face her sister. 'You were the fool, Mall, for it could have been you. For so long you had the greatest Prince in Christendom in your thrall and made not the slightest use of it. Do not dare to argue now with what I shall do with the same power you had and threw away. You were what you have always been — a fool too eager to please, but not I.'

Mary swayed and caught at the chair for support, her senses reeling. Anne raged on.

'I shall rule Henry and thus England and my every whim shall be law, while you, poor simpleton, will be but a country squire's wife, hard put to it to pay your servants and replenish your linen.' For a second she paused, then shrewd black eyes peered closely at the wan face before her, and Mary's vacant gaze as she slumped into a chair.

'And too poor to hire a wet-nurse,' she added, 'for it seems to me you are with child. Is it so, Mall?'

Mary started, staring up at the curious dark eyes in horror. 'I, with child? Oh no, it cannot be!'

CHAPTER TWENTY

BERCEUSE

THE doubt that Anne had raised in Mary's mind persisted long after Anne had gone. Could it be that the dizziness and nausea of the past weeks betokened more than shock and grief? Could it possibly be that she was carrying a child? If so, Mary realised with dismay, it would be nigh impossible to determine whose child she bore. At last, unable to bear the secret fear alone, she confided in Lady Beth.

'The symptoms sound highly like pregnancy,' the wise old lady pronounced, having listened without comment to Mary's troubled tale. 'But since the child could as well be Will Carey's as the King's, there is naught to fear, my lamb. The babe will be born here and I shall care for you. I doubt not your husband will be delighted.' For Lady Beth life was always simple and uncomplicated, Mary thought with a tinge of envy. But secret fear nagged. If the coming babe was Henry's son, he should be told of it, surely?

Will Carey was emphatic. 'Why complicate matters further for yourself, Mall? Do you think the King would feel beholden to you or take you back when he is so besotted with your sister? Far more likely, if he recognises the child, that he will take it as he took Bess Blount's son from her, and bring him up at Court. Would you lose your child thus, Mary?'

'No, Will, oh no!' she cried, clinging to Will's arm in terror at the prospect.

'Then it is settled.' Will's voice, though low, was firm

and commanding. 'Though I have never forced myself upon you, I have exercised a husband's rights when you granted me. The babe might well be my child. I tell you now, sweetheart, the babe *is* mine, and since you have left Court there is no need to announce that you are with child. Bide you here and rest and recover your strength, beloved, for you will need all you can muster by the time the babe is born.'

Reassured, Mary watched the tall, erect figure of her husband ride out of the courtyard to return to his Court duties. He was a fine man, this Will Carey, and she felt the dull, shrunken thing that was her aching heart begin to swell and fill out again a little with admiration and respect. And as the months slipped slowly by her optimistic nature began to reassert itself as Mary counted her blessings.

For many years she had held the King's heart, far more than any mortal woman could have expected. And now, far from being left desserted and unloved, she was still secure in the love of a fine man, though far more lowly and humble than Henry. Slowly but surely the heartache receded, leaving Mary resigned.

'Approaching motherhood has such a softening effect,' Lady Beth observed sagely. 'Once you have your own babe in your arms to love and nurture, naught else will trouble you, child. Contentment will come again.'

Only Sir Thomas's quick, brief visits to Hever ruffled the incipient calm that was descending over it.

'My clever daughter Anne fares well,' he enthused to Lady Beth while Mary sat silent, still hugging her secret close. Lady Beth had promised not to reveal the advent of a grandchild to Sir Thomas yet, lest he guess its father and plot accordingly . . .

'Yes, Anne is the shrewd child she ever was,' he went on, rubbing his thin, acquisitive hands together eagerly before the fire. 'She knows how to bait her fish and play him well before landing him, and holding His Grace at bay affords us all great favours. Not a Howard nor a Boleyn can help but prosper while the King and Wolsey plan the divorce and Anne is still beyond reach. What a wise child she is, so clever, so hard a bargain-driver she almost puts me to shame.'

Lady Beth glanced in agitation at her other stepdaughter sitting by the fireside with her sewing, fearful lest Thomas's short memory of Mary's role as the King's mistress should wound her. But Mary was thinking only of how changeable Father was; not so very long ago he had been attempting to match Anne with her Irish cousin and reviling her for her refusal. Now she was his favoured child again.

Carey brought word of how Henry still pursued and pined for the elusive Anne, and on her sister's next visit Mary reproached her gently for causing Henry such torment.

Anne laughed sardonically. 'He shall fret as I have done before and shall never do again. He say pay for others' sins.'

'Could you not have pity and love him — just a little?' Mary besought her. 'Henry is such a lonely man. He needs love.'

'Needs my body, you mean. But I am not a creature for furtiveness, Mall. Nor shall I prostitute myself to him.'

'As I did? But I loved him, Nan.'

'And do still if I am not mistaken. Does he know yet of the child?'

She glanced down meaningfully at her sister's burgeoning stomach.

'No, Nan, and I beg you do not tell him. This babe is Will's and mine and no affair of the King's.'

'Say you so?' Anne's smile was amused. 'Then so be it, and I shall not say differently.'

'And will you soften to Henry?'

'Become his harlot? Never! I have told him I give myself

to my husband and none other, and soon it shall be, Mall. Wolsey begins the divorce proceedings soon.'

'Then you do love him a little?'

'Not in the least. But I plan to stay here in Hever until Henry is distracted for want of me. That, I think, will make matters move a little faster.'

Gifts and letters began to pour into the castle daily. Anne flaunted Henry's letters proudly.

'I and my heart put ourselves in your hands,' he wrote. 'The pain of absence already is too great . . . it would be almost intolerable were it not for my firm hope of your unchanging affection for me.' Anne smiled contentedly. 'It cannot be long now, Mall.' Mary turned away to hide the smart. Never had Henry written thus to her.

Then suddenly Mary was in labour. Lady Beth and Anne hustled to and fro, both white-faced and anxious as Mary sweated and moaned throughout the night. In the grey light of dawn a first thin squeal pierced the twilight air, and Mary saw Anne standing by with a white-swaddled bundle while Lady Beth busied herself over Mary's sweat-soaked, enervated body.

Anne's dark eyes peered closely at the child.

'A son, Mall,' she whispered.

'And he is well?' Mary's voice sounded thin and faint even to herself.

'He is beautiful. Fair and ruddy and strong with the most beautiful blue eyes I ever saw.' The note in Anne's voice was tender. Lady Beth, her task ended, brushed back the hairs escaping from her cap and went forward eagerly.

'Let me see, Nan.' She took the bundle and brought it close to the candle by the bedside where Mary could see. The babe's russet-gold hair and small blue eyes screwed in angry screaming were a tiny replica of Henry in a rage, and Mary's heart turned over. He was undoubtedly Henry's child. Instantly sorrow filled her. Poor Will, he would be so saddened.

'The image of his father,' said Anne stoutly. 'Will Carey will be a proud man indeed to have a son with the same fair colouring and handsome features. Come, Mother, let us put him down to sleep now while Mary rests.'

She smiled at her sister before leaving, and Mary could have wept for joy. It was true. The babe could well pass for Will's, and Anne would stolidly uphold his paternity. Henry would not rob her of her child after all. A new peace stole over her as she drifted into sleep.

With a flurry of hoofbeats and a clatter of footsteps on the staircase Will was home, his face almost beatific with pleasure to behold his wife and son. As he held the child in his arms not a flicker of any emotion save delight crossed his handsome face.

'My son,' he murmured. 'Mary, I am so proud of you.' Laying the child down in its cradle he came closer, kneeling by the bedside, his voice choking with emotion. 'Dearest wife, I love you as I have loved you long, and I am proud to call you wife. I only beg to be allowed always to love and cherish you and our son, and I ask not your love in return, only the freedom to love you.' He buried his face in the counterpane. Mary's hand stroked the fine gold hair, and a rush of emotion filled her veins.

'I think I have always loved you too, Will, though I am slow of wit, as I have always been told, and have only come to know of it lately.' His gaze lifted, his blue eyes disbelieving. 'It is true, Will Carey. I love you and wish for naught else but you and our son, and Anne may seek all she will if I am granted this.'

He moaned, covering her hand with kisses, but she knew she had given him now some of the happiness he had granted her. Dear, loyal Will. It was true, she wanted now nothing else but the peace and security of a constant love, and with Will and the babe it would be hers.

'How shall we name our son, Will?'

He stood, holding her hand still tightly in his. 'He shall

be named Henry,' he pronounced firmly. 'Henry Carey — it has a fine ring to it.'

Mary felt a catch in her throat. It was Will's last gesture to her love for Henry the King, a noble gesture.

'Thank you,' she said simply.

Soon Will returned to Placentia and life at Hever became a peaceful routine once again. But all bitterness and nostalgia was gone now Mary had a lusty son to care for, and the days passed contentedly. The arrival of letters for Anne from the King no longer disturbed Mary but they brought Anne little happiness either.

'I would matters were resolved,' she commented moodily after the latest gift had arrived. 'So long this divorce drags on! I almost envy you, Mall, in your maternal peace. Like a broody hen you concern yourself with naught but your husband and child. Oh, to be content with simple things!'

'I am but a simple creature,' Mary replied.

'And the happier for it. I sometimes wonder where my restless, searching nature will lead me. I wonder if I have embarked on the right course after all.'

The token she was sending Henry, a jewel in the form of a storm-tossed maiden, was a symbol of the uncertainty of her future, she told Mary as she showed her the jewel. Mary felt a sudden shiver of apprehension. Into what danger was Anne betraying herself, she wondered fearfully. God grant Anne in her cleverness could see clearly where she was leading herself, for Mary's wits could not.

Abruptly Anne decided to answer Henry's plea for her to return to Court. Hever was strangely quiet when she was gone, but for Mary every day was full and happy. Baby Harry grew and thrived, and soon he was shuffling unsteadily on plump little feet about the passages and chambers.

Spring, summer, autumn and winter came and passed and then again, and Mary and Will found immeasurable contentment in their union and in their son. So far removed did the false glitter of Court seem now to Mary that she heard almost with surprise occasionally of Anne's activities. Little seemed to happen. Anne apparently still held the half-crazed Henry at bay while Wolsey still struggled to secure the King's divorce.

Then death swept Wolsey from the scene, just as Anne was about to demand his execution of Henry.

'Strange,' Carey commented laconically. 'She has hated Wolsey for many years. Now she is to receive his palace, York House, as a gift from the King.'

The palace he once promised me, Mary mused, but the thought caused her no pain.

Time went on. The news that the King had banished Queen Catherine from Court and kept Anne close by his side while the battle for his divorce still raged, caused little comment at Hever.

In time came word that at last the King's divorce was settled. One day in the New Year 1533 Sir Thomas Boleyn, now Earl of Wiltshire, came galloping to Hever, near-demented with joy, and almost fell over his grandson as he entered. He picked up the child, now a sturdy five-year-old, and cradled Harry to him.

'Beth, there is news! The divorce is agreed and Anne is to marry the King! His Grace has created Anne Marquess of Pembroke, and even now they return from a visit to France, where she was received by King Francis himself as though she were already Queen. We shall be the most powerful family in the land! Is that not splendid news?'

'Wonderful, husband,' Lady Beth echoed, her voice faint with bewilderment. 'But let me take Harry — he is dribbling his quince on your doublet.'

'His Grace and Anne are coming here tomorrow, so bid the servants hasten to prepare.'

'At once, husband. And is Will coming too?'

'Sir Thomas clicked his tongue testily. 'I expect so, but

hasten, wife. They come but for one day.'

Mary saw the glance Lady Beth threw in her direction and knew her meaning.

'I shall make myself scarce, Father, when His Grace comes if you will permit,' she said quietly.

'As you will,' he retorted quickly. Mary's past role and present feelings were of little account now when so magnificent a future spread itself beckoningly before the Boleyns.

Thankfully Mary planned to take Harry and walk as far from the Castle as they could, taking food so they could remain away until Henry and Anne were safely gone. Beyond the village, far along the banks of the Eden should be safe, she judged. Then another thought arrested her; suppose Anne misinterpreted her absence? She could believe it was because Mary objected to her marrying the King, or worse still, was jealous. She was not to know that it was the cherubic, ruddy face of Mary's son Harry with his telltale lively eyes and Tudor-gold hair which made it imperative to remove him from the King's sight lest he should guess.

Taking quill and paper Mary seated herself and began to write.

'Sweet sister,' Mary scratched painstakingly. 'Far from scorn or jealousy I feel only love and concern for you, and wish with all my heart that the road that now stretches before you will lead to happiness. I say this lest you misconstrue my absence, but I deem it wisest not to meet again with His Grace while I live.

'That I have lost his love I know, but no longer does it chafe my heart, contented as I am in the love of a good man. That you may find the same contentment with your noble spouse I would speak to you of those traits I learned of him, though you are wise beyond aught I could attain.

'His determination you know, else you would not be about to wear a crown. His love of luxury and pleasure likewise, and his power to charm with his quick cleverness and melting ways. But on the darker side of the Sun, he is not a happy man, searching always for what he cannot find, restless and changeable. To interfere with what he seeks brings instant thunder, for he is tenacious and fiercely aggressive, and his rages bring terror to all. There is in him also that which fears without knowing what he fears, a sense of foreboding which causes him acute terror at times and he broods incessantly. When thus troubled, His Grace seeks only the comfort of warm and tender arms, of a love which questions not. Above all he seeks love and admiration, as a child seeks to please its elders. Comfort him, Anne, cross him not. I have a fear your nature, as powerful and resolute as his own, could lead you to mischief if you are unwise.

'Scold me not, dear sister, that I write these words. It is only your good fortune that I wish, and while you bear with Henry's weaknesses and remember that he is a vulnerable creature, prone to tempers and belated remorse, you will prosper. Only drive him not, for Henry will not be coerced.

'The child beneath Henry's manly body is a sweet and petulant thing. Care for him well, for he has sore need of a woman's love. May God's blessing go with you both, and I crave you destroy this screed. Your loving sister, Mall.'

The letter sealed, Mary entrusted it to Lady Beth with the admonition to give it to Anne only when she was alone. That done, Mary called Harry to her, and with a basket of food, they set out. To her relief the boy did not question why they walked so far from Hever on a winter's day, with the trees stripped of leaves and the woods bereft of birdsong. Happily he skipped along before her, skimming stones across the stream and laughing at the ripples.

They were beyond the village when the sound of horns came echoing over the barren fields, distant but clear on the crisp December air. Henry and Anne were arriving at Hever Castle.

CHAPTER TWENTY ONE

CODA

PALE sunlight filtered feebly through the stark branches of the trees along the riverbank as their footsteps carried Mary and her son far from the castle. On the far fringe of the village some children played at the water's edge and their round eyes watched the coming of the finely-dressed strangers with curiosity.

Confidently Harry went to join them, talking animatedly to them in his desire to attract their company. How like Henry he was, Mary thought involuntarily, so eager for admiring company and with the same facility to charm with his pleasing manner and easy smile. Even the jaunty stride and proud bearing were those of a King.

Mary seated herself on a fallen tree bough to watch the children at play, laying aside her basket and drawing her fur-lined cloak closer about her shoulders. At her age one had to take care if one did not wish to creak rheumatically through the rest of the winter. How strange, the thought, to be thirty-four already, and it scarce seemed a summer's breath ago since she was nineteen and Henry's new love. Yet in the space of sixteen years she had lapsed from King's mistress to squire's wife, though plump and comely still, and seen her sister take her place at the King's side. Mary smiled wryly. She would not have it otherwise now. Will would be content when he heard the news she had to tell him.

'Harry, have a care for your hose!' The boy was scrambling with catlike agility to the topmost branch of a denuded tree, the youngsters below watching admiringly.

Mary's maternal eyes followed his ascent and so absorbed was she that she heard no footstep or crackling twigs behind her. A sudden, resonant voice made her start.

'Mistress Mary?'

She turned, a hand half-raised in alarm, and saw Henry standing there, his head tilted at a questioning angle and a smile lighting his rosy, wind-whipped cheeks as he saw it was indeed Mary. Tall still, but broader than she remembered him, he seemed to fill the landscape in his magnificent green and silver-slashed doublet and hose, his cloak blowing back from his immense shoulders in the breeze.

'May I sit with you?' Without waiting for an answer Henry pulled off his jewelled cap and seated himself at her side on the tree-trunk. Mary stared at him, too surprised to speak. Golden-haired and golden-bearded he looked magnificent still, but she could not help noticing with a tinge of regret that the hair was thinning now and his jowl heavier, causing his eyes to look smaller still in the folds of flesh. He too was ageing. At forty-two he had begun to acquire the thickened body of middle age despite his constant athletic activity. No wonder Anne did not find the monarch as physically fascinating as Mary had done. Henry was still smiling quizzically.

'Are you not pleased to see me, Mary, after so long?'

Mary lowered her eyes; she had been staring most impolitely. 'You took me by surprise, Sire. I did not expect to meet anyone here today.'

'I wanted to see you, to tell you I am to marry your sister after all. In a few days' time we shall be married at Whitehall.'

'Whitehall?'

'The new name I have given to York Place. I wanted to see you again, Mall, to thank you and to know you are content.'

'Then you may return satisfied, Sire, for I am content.'

'You are faring well then with Carey?'

Mary looked directly into the small, curious blue eyes. 'You did me the greatest service of all, Sire, when you chose me Will Carey to wed. He is a fine husband and father.'

She could have bitten her tongue in vexation. With her usual tactlessness and lack of guile she had let slip that which she had not wished him to know. Henry's quick mind did not miss the clue.

'Father? Then you have borne him children, Mall?'

'Aye, a son. And soon, I hope, another, though he knows not of it yet.'

It took great effort not to look across the field at the son she loved so proudly. One close look and Henry would know at once whose child he was. But Henry was gazing at her in admiration.

'I am delighted, Mall, and hope all Boleyns prove as fruitful, for you know how long I have prayed God for a son to rule England after me. All these years I have been cheated and disappointed, but now, Mall, now I begin to hope . . .'

His gaze grew misty and the small eyes wandered from her face away across the field to where the children squealed at play. Mary grew curious.

'You hope, Sire?'

'Anne is with child, she believes, and that is why we marry swiftly. My son must be legitimate. He *will* be legitimate, I will have it so. He will be strong and lusty and a natural leader of men.'

His gaze rested on the leader of the far group of youngsters. 'That is a fine boy yonder,' he commented idly. 'Agile and courageous — see how the others stand silent in awe? Who is he, do you know?'

For the first time in her life Mary deliberately lied. 'A village boy I think, Sire. And I sincerely hope with you, Your Grace, that Anne bears you such sons as you so earnestly desire.'

He turned the pale blue gaze keenly on her. 'Then you bear me no malice, Mary, for what has passed between us?'

She smiled warmly. 'None, Sire. For me only good came of it, and I wish with all my heart that Anne too will find as great contentment.'

'Then come, let us return to the castle where you may felicitate her yourself, for we must not tarry overlong. Anne and I must return to London forthwith.' He rose, extending his hand to take hers, but Mary shook her head.

'Go you back alone, Sire, and I shall return later. I wish you God speed, and pray give Anne my love and earnest wishes.'

'I shall.' He turned to go, then paused and turned to her again. 'Sweet Mall, so comforting and welcoming always, if ever there is aught you want of me ...'

'There is naught, Your Grace. I have all I wish in the world,' Mary interrupted proudly then, rising and sweeping a low curtsey, she indicated as clearly as if she had spoken the words aloud that she had done with him. Henry stood, irresolute, for a second.

'Then I shall send Carey out to meet you,' he said curtly, and strode away. Watching his retreating figure Mary felt a wave of sadness engulf her, but it was not regret for a lost love but an undefinable sense of foreboding for Anne. After so many years of keeping him dangling she had realised at length that her only hope of retaining him was to submit to his embrace. And now she was with child, apparently. God grant it was a boy-child, or that Anne bore another boy before too late, for she was already thirty-two. Henry was an evil person to frusstrate and Anne's failure could only mean dire misfortune. Mary shivered involuntarily. A chubby arm encircled her neck.

'Can we eat now, Mother, for I am starving?' The blue-eyed gaze of the child was so like that of the adult one so recently seated here that Mary did not answer for a moment. At least Henry had not recognised his son. Her world of Will and Harry was still secure, and with God's grace there would soon be a fourth member of her beloved family to increase her happiness.

Harry plucked her sleeve. 'Please, Mother?'

'Of course. Sit here by me.'

Presently there came the sound of distant hoofbeats and a trumpet call, the signal of Anne and Henry's departure. Gathering up her basket, Mary rose and called to Harry that it was time to return before dusk fell.

A tall, slender figure came striding across the meadows towards them as they walked, and Mary recognised with a leap of pleasure the outline of Will Carey's eager figure. Sweeping both Mary and the child into one fervent embrace, Will's handsome features were evidence enough of his delight at their reunion.

'How goes it with you, Mary my love? Are you well?' he asked softly, brown eyes raking her face anxiously.

'Well, husband, and the better for seeing you,' she answered with a smile.

'I believe His Grace spoke with you before he left?'

'He did. A final farewell, Will, but do not fret over it. There is no love in Henry for me nor in me for him now, though I wish him well.'

'I fret for nothing, Mall. I rejoice in my good fortune that I have you — and the boy there.' He glanced affectionately at Harry who was skipping ahead of them. 'But before I forget — I have a letter for you from Anne, written secretly while the King sought you. She bade me give it you privily.' He drew the missive from his sleeve. 'Read it now, if you will, while I talk with Harry.'

He strode quickly ahead to join the child while Mary lingered to read in the fading light.

'Dear sister,' went Anne's firm, clear handwriting, 'My heart is conscious of the goodwill and love you bear me and conscious therefore of a tremor of regret that my good fortune must be your loss. But since you express yourself content with your lot I am absolved, I think, of any guilt that I chose to take Henry of England from your bed and now welcome him to mine.

'Know then, sister, that I did not choose Henry with my heart but with the Boleyn acumen that was born in me. God willing, however, I may come to love him, if only for the sake of the child I believe I am to bear him.

'You counsel wisely though I need not fear. Henry worships me as no goddess was ever idolised before, heaping me with gifts and jewels. Because of me the most powerful fall, even the Queen, Catherine, languishes in The More, deposed for me. The laws of the land are changed, and all who would defy me are swiftly put down; even the very course of the Church in England, once thought immutable, is altering because of me. Though yet uncrowned, my power is greater than that of any Queen before me.

'Life is strange, sweet sister, for had you wished it that power could have been yours. Between us we two sisters have enslaved the greatest monarch in Christendon this dozen years and more, and while you scorned to avail yourself, I have seized the opportunity which leads me to my wedding with the King in Whitehall on St. Paul's Day.

'Thereafter will follow my Coronation, Mall, and the public acclaim and recognition for which I have always been destined. I would grieve for your obscurity but that you assure me you are content. God grant it may always be so.

'Fret no more for me, Mall, for I go to great and glorious matters. Never will regret cloud my days, for I know I choose aright. Your letter burns now in the fire, whither I beg this presently may follow.

Nan.'

A smile of sadness flickered gently on Mary's lips when Will returned to her side. Somehow Anne's confidence left her doubtful and unconvinced, but for once she hoped her intuition was wrong. The days of Henry with his Mistress of the Moonlight had been carefree, golden days of happiness, and Mary prayed inwardly that the days of the Mistress of the Midnight would prove no less fortuitous for Anne.

Will's arm slid reassuringly under hers. 'All is well, I trust, Mall?'

'All is very well, dear husband — for us at least. It is for Anne I fear.'

Will's laugh was harsh, abrupt. 'She deserves not your compassion, sweetheart, for she baits the King only for what she can obtain from his idiotic passion. A King's mistress evokes pity in no one.'

Mary looked up shyly. 'Yet for years you knew I was Henry's mistress, Will, but never once have you reproached me.'

Will stopped, putting his hands on her shoulders and gazing directly down into her eyes. 'Nor ever will, sweet wife, for always your love is freely given and asks naught in return. Who can accuse a sinner of loving too well? Your sister now, she bargains like a whorehouse wench and cannot prosper. God help her, is all I can say of Mistress Anne, for surely no one else will.'

Tears clouded Mary's eyes. 'I am sorry Mall, I did not mean to hurt you,' Will whispered, his voice choked with remorse. 'I meant only to point the difference between you, why you are loved and she is not. I would not hurt you for the world, sweetheart, you whom I love above aught else, save Harry.'

He called the child to them, and the three figures crossed the darkening greensward before Hever Castle to where lights already glowed in the windows.

'You do not return to Greenwich yet, husband? You may stay with us the night?' she asked anxiously, suddenly conscious of his duties.

Will smiled and hugged her closer. 'His Grace has given me leave to stay a week with you.'

'Then I am glad, husband, for there is news I would tell

you which must not be broken lightly. It deserves time, and privacy,' she mused, thinking already of the vast bed, curtained off like an island from the prying eyes of the world. And in her mind's eye already she could foresee the glow of delight which would irradiate her husband's face.

No, not for anything in the world would she change places with Anne, soon to be Queen of England. Halcyon though the days with Henry would always remain in her memory, undoubtedly obscurity and peace were infinitely to be preferred to glittering prominence.

Author's Note

Contrary to general belief, I am of the opinion that it was Mary as the elder sister and not Anne Boleyn who travelled to France in 1514 in the train of the Princess Mary Rose. I believe Anne did in fact go to France for an education and was later introduced by her father to the Court of Queen Claude. The letter still extant from Anne to her father (referred to on page 73) is generally held to refer to his introducing her to the Court of Queen Catherine in England, but to me it is more feasible that she refers to Queen Claude. For this interpretation I am indebted to J.J. Gardner's article 'Mary and Anne Boleyn' which appeared in the English Historical Review, Vol. 8, 1893.

That Mary bore a son named Henry, later Lord Hunsdon, is fact, but whether he was her husband's child or the King's is still disputed. He could well have been Henry's son born at the end of a long affair with Mary which persisted while Anne still held him at arm's length.

Scorned by her father and brother because of her docile, unambitious nature, Mary was renounced by them on marrying the obscure Carey. Rightfully the heir to Sir Thomas Boleyn's estates on his death since Anne and her brother George had been executed, she was nevertheless deprived of any right to inherit, for King Henry seized Hever Castle and the other Boleyn estates in his dead wife Anne's name after her execution in 1531.